Murc

Pamel

This book is dedicated to my son, Stewart, and his wonderful family.

PROLOGUE

'Hello?' she called out in the darkness. 'Is anybody there?' The only sound was the echo of her own voice, then deadly silence. Maybe she'd been mistaken, but she was almost certain that there'd been a sound coming from over in the far corner of the warehouse. Although not of a nervous disposition, Jennifer Grayson had always felt a degree of discomfort when closing up for the night when the only source of light came from the green illuminated exit sign next to the door at the back of the building. Franklin Electronics in Boldon Business Park, Tyne and Wear, was one of those rare companies who had never had a break-in. This was probably due to the high degree of security installed on the premises, one the owner had paid an arm and a leg for, as she recalled. It included a security guard patrolling the perimeter every couple of hours so statistically there was really very little chance of a break-in ever happening.

Maybe it had just been a noise from the outside of the building. John, the security guard, would be starting his shift right about now, and it could have easily been him parking up and closing the car door behind him before walking past the part of the warehouse she was in now, on his way to the porta cabin at the front of the building.

She put that down as the answer and breathed a huge sigh of relief. She chastised herself for even thinking that anyone could get in here in the first place. It was extremely unlikely; the building didn't have public access at all, but was a closed warehouse with offices. If not John moving about outside then it was probably one of the many boxes in there settling, as she knew that they sometimes did. Surely that was all it could possibly be?

The company had thrived in the last few years, and its range of electronic goods was in demand not only in the UK but also in Europe, where a subsidiary company had been set-up to handle delivery throughout the continent. Just over a year ago, Jennifer had been appointed deputy European manager, and had even travelled abroad with her colleague, John Scott, who was head of European distribution, to oversee everything... with all expenses paid too.

Even so, when her turn came on the rota to close shop for the night, she always had this niggling feeling in the back of her mind that there was a possibility, even though it was a highly unlikely one, that anyone could have somehow crept into the premises and hid in one of the many corners behind the boxes. And they could have remained there until all the staff had gone. Then they could have a field day amongst the stock and make off with whatever they wanted. Jennifer was fully aware that Christmas was coming up, and anyone of a thieving disposition would steal anything they could get their hands on to sell for cash either on the Internet, or even to family and friends, as long as they could get a good source of income out of what they'd pilfered. Or they could keep the goods for themselves, if that was what they'd been stolen for. *A nice little Christmas gift for somebody,* she thought. *How many people actually ask online if what they are buying is genuinely owned by the seller?* But there again, her imagination had gone into overdrive. As she was one of the three keyholders and therefore responsible for ensuring everything was all safely and securely closed down for the night, she didn't want to be the one to let the company down by being lax and not doing her job properly. She valued her job; jobs were hard to come by in these parts, and she'd been very lucky in getting such a good one with great pay and benefits.

Then she heard it again; a clank from the same corner. Jennifer reached inside her bag for the torch she always carried with her on these dark evenings. It was an invaluable accessory when trying to get her car key in the lock. She'd suffered too many scratches on the paintwork in the past with her fumbling about in the darkness. On this occasion, she was glad it was there.

The torch lit up the darkness when she slid the on button across, and she pointed it towards the corner where she thought she'd heard the noise coming from. Thick dust particles fluttered through the beam. A warehouse filled with boxes was never going to be one of the cleanest of places on the face of the earth, but as long as what was in the boxes was protected, that was all that mattered. Still nothing. She felt reluctant to go any closer but felt obliged to do so. Taking a deep breath, she moved to where she thought she'd heard the noise.

Heart now pounding, she shone the torch down the space behind the row of boxes, and was filled with such an overwhelming relief to find nothing there.

In truth, she had no idea what she would have done if she'd found anyone lurking there behind them. She really should have found the time to get her phone out beforehand and punched in the numbers 999 so she was ready to press the green call button if need be. Her quickened heartbeat began to slowly subside and she laughed nervously to herself.

'Idiot!' she said, turning to go. As she made her way to the exit, the sound of her shoes seemed to suddenly echo on the concrete behind her. Her blood chilled as she realised that someone was following her and she quickly reached in her bag to find her phone. As she was rummaging around, she felt something being forced against the backs of her calves and she fell awkwardly to the ground.

Her head hit the concrete and pain exploded all down the left-hand side of her face. She could feel the swelling start almost immediately around her eye and cheek. With the wind taken out of her and unable to shout out or even move, she could only lie and listen to what happened next. There was an odd metallic sound, as if something made of steel was being scraped along the ground, then a sharp, sudden burning pain unlike anything else she had ever felt in her life. Then darkness...

Her head lay a few feet away, face up, blank eyes staring into space. After giving it a fleeting glance, the attacker flicked something into the widening pool of blood that had now almost surrounded her body, then walked towards the illuminated exit sign at the far end of the warehouse and out into the cold evening air.

1
***

Detective Inspector Joe Burton and his partner, Detective Sergeant Sally Fielding, were sitting in his car downing the remnants of the coffees they'd bought at a drive-through Costa about ten minutes previously, when the call came through. It had been a couple of hours since they'd agreed it had already been a long day. This had been their second pit stop of the evening at this particular watering hole. Not too far from the Greater Manchester Police Headquarters on Northampton Road, it was ideally situated for a quick pull-in, order their beverages on the crackling microphone, and then pick up the drinks at the next window. It was one they'd frequented more times than they cared to think about, and not only when they'd been out and about in the car.

'Beats station coffee,' Burton declared every time he took the first sip of his now regular caffeine fix, and Fielding couldn't disagree with that sentiment. It was worth every penny of the fortune they'd just paid for it, despite the fact that they could have easily bought several jars of instant with the same amount of money. Burton's regular coffee of choice was a double espresso latte, occasionally with the added delights of a hazelnut or gingerbread flavouring depending on the season, and hers a regular cappuccino with a hefty dusting of chocolate on the top.

Truth be told, she would have settled with a cup full of the thick, creamy froth that came with that particular choice of drink as she probably loved that just as much as the coffee itself. 'It's supposed to be a topping and not the actual drink or face decoration!' he had teased her whenever she took a sip and saw that she had more of it on her top lip than in her mouth. This was the nectar of the gods by comparison to what they served up in the canteen or dispensed from the drinks machines at work. *What was the best term to describe the station coffee? Could it even be called coffee*, she thought to herself. *A better term would be pigswill!*

Despite their being DI and DS respectively, Burton and Fielding were friends in addition to being partnered detectives. It was a friendship which had steadily built up over the last seven years they had been assigned to one another. Fielding only referred to her superior officer as "sir" when operating in their official capacity, otherwise it was simply "Joe".

Although she had lived and worked in Manchester for the past thirteen years, Fielding was born and bred in the north east of England in a little semi-rural village called Boldon, midway between the cities of Sunderland and Newcastle and the seaside town of South Shields. Her father, a police officer, had died of a heart attack while on duty when she was a mere sixteen-year-old.

When Fielding had declared to her mother that she intended to follow in her father's footsteps after her A-levels, all hell broke loose. Fielding never spoke to either her mother or her elder sister again.

With a temperament more in tune with her father's, rather than her mother's or sibling's, she knew her own mind and what she wanted to achieve – and if that meant alienating herself from her family, then so be it. She hoped they would eventually come around, but sadly, in her thirteen years away from them, neither had come around to understanding – or wanting to understand – her way of thinking. In fact, there had been no contact whatsoever. After all this time, giving in and making contact seemed to her to be out of the question, as the longer they had waited the more impossible it would be to do. Neither, it seemed, could swallow their pride and make the first move.

She had seen her sister's name a few times in newspapers and in some of the glossy home decorating magazines, and she'd even seen her on television a couple of times on those reality makeover shows, but that was as near as she had got to either of them. As her dad had originally come from Manchester and had relatives in and around the area, she had applied to Manchester's Police College and left the nest as quickly as she could take flight from it, finding solace with her new-found family down there. They had all welcomed her into the fold and supported her in her choice of career – unlike her mother and sister.

Thirty-eight-year-old Joe Burton had also moved to Manchester from his native roots. Originally hailing from north London, he and his then long-term partner had moved up to the Midlands eight years ago when she had successfully applied for and gained a very lucrative promotion within her financial consultancy firm. Even though it had meant uprooting themselves from the lovely little house that they'd made for themselves in Muswell Hill, Burton hadn't minded changing cities and simply made an internal application with the force to make the move further north.

He'd made some good friends in his home town and would certainly miss them, but knew that he'd make more again when he'd settled in his new home in Manchester. He was the sort of man who was good at making friends with people. Everything had been rosy at first, and life was better than good until his partner decided to play footsie and then house with another colleague of hers – and that was that.

The split had been immediate. Burton wasn't going to be made a fool of, and had thrown himself into his job. He swore that he would never allow himself to be in that position again. Despite having the odd girlfriend now and then, which were, more often than not, blind dates set-up for him by concerned friends and work colleagues anxious to see him happily settled down, he never allowed himself to fully trust another woman again. His partnership with Fielding was the closest he had come to any sort of relationship over the past seven years.

During this time, they had successfully tackled some of the hardest cases known to either of them, and had gained unending praise from their superiors along the way. But the case they had just finished working on had been a long and particularly arduous one, and had taken up nearly all of their resources. Finding the motive for the murder of a young homeless man living on the city's streets had turned out to be a very unusual and bizarre case. It had finally been cracked wide open yesterday, thanks to the great detective work and joint efforts of their entire team. Although they were very much a young team of detectives, Burton knew that what they perhaps lacked in age they certainly made up for in enthusiasm and dogged determination. They tackled anything that he threw at them head-on, never giving up or letting go until they'd reached a successful conclusion – no matter what. He perhaps didn't tell them as often as he should have done, but he was extremely proud of all of them.

Today had been mainly tidying up and completing paperwork. Plus, they could finally release the body to the man's family. Their celebratory cup of coffee marked the end of a trying few weeks on a case which had proved to be more emotionally stressful than usual. It also marked the end of their shift for the day. Buying a coffee had become the norm for them each evening before heading off to their homes.

Weeknights on duty in Manchester's city centre were relatively quiet ones. It was the Friday and Saturday night shifts that were the worst when the hardcore binge drinkers came out, and not all of them of the male variety either these days, as a steadily increasing number of female drinkers seemed to be competing with their male counterparts. Burton and Fielding had seen it all: from the skimpily clad ladies of the hen night party and the boisterous testosterone-fuelled stag night posse, the latter all macho and muscles, to the regular weekend drinkers out looking for – and always finding – a fight with either another of a like mind or with some poor unsuspecting sod who either said something they didn't like or just looked at them in a funny way. *Fight Club*... for real... not tucked away in some underground lair but alive and well and living on the streets of Manchester.

Alcohol, thought Burton, *nectar of idiots. A few bevvies in and all sense leaves the building.* He felt sorry for the on-duty uniformed officers caught in the crossfire outside the city's many pubs, clubs and wine bars, with fists and expletives flying all around them for most of the evening while they tried to maintain some modicum of peace against all odds. Along with Fielding, he had, on more than one occasion, found himself caught up in the drinkers' affray, coming away with bumps and bruises and even, on a couple of occasions, a fractured rib or two. Funny, neither of them remembered it ever being like that when they were young and out on the town.

Fielding wasn't a heavy drinker anyway, and only ever on special occasions. And despite Burton's own relationship disaster in the past when he could have easily sat and drowned his sorrows, he just didn't feel the need to resort to alcohol to the same degree as these hardened drinkers did. A couple of beers now and again perhaps, but not to the extent that he didn't know either where he was or even who he was. That was just stupid in his mind, and a complete waste of money.

So, when their police radio crackled into action and a dispatcher's voice addressed them personally, they were taken completely off guard. Why on earth would there be any calls patched through to them as they'd already signed off their shift and informed dispatch before leaving the station twenty minutes earlier?

'We're off duty!' Burton had bellowed into the communication system's handset he picked up from the car's dashboard, giving Fielding such a surprise that she gave him a sideways look and a raised eyebrow. Surely they weren't being called out to separate a few over-enthusiastic Hallowe'en drinkers? There were plenty of on-duty police constables on the beat available for that.

'I'm sorry, sir,' the dispatcher apologised. 'I know that you are, but there's nobody else available at the moment, and the detective chief inspector has asked for a team of detectives to attend a possible crime scene as soon as possible.'

'There must be somebody else available at the station. Can't you get in touch with them? We're just about home.' Burton lied about the last bit but pushed to try to get another pair of detectives to attend the scene, knowing that both himself and Fielding had already gone way over their shift finish time.

'Like I said, sir,' the voice continued amid the crackles, his deter-mination showing, 'I've already tried and you're the only ones I can get in contact with.'

Sighing just loud enough for the man to hear, he looked at Fielding and she nodded. One last trip out. Surely it wouldn't take that long?

'Okay then,' he finally agreed, thinking someone owed him big on this one. 'What's the address?' Expecting it to be somewhere in the city centre, more than likely a popular watering hole or night-club where an affray would start up without any reason at all, he was more than surprised to discover their destination to be a care home in Middleton just about a mile away from where they were now.

They could see the glow of the flashing blue lights of the police vehicles in the distance even before they reached the road the care home was in. A solitary uniformed police officer standing on the pavement by the entrance to the driveway looked like he had his hands full holding back the small but exuberant crowd that had gathered around him when they arrived. They had probably been drawn there by the flashing lights and the increased police activity on the scene, and also out of morbid curiosity as to what was going on in the building beyond the dense leylandii hedging. Maybe they thought that they'd catch a glimpse of a dead body or two – as highly unlikely as that would be.

Pulling up by the side of the road, Burton and Fielding showed the police officer their warrant cards. He nodded for them to go on up through the gates to the house, undoing one side of the police barrier tape for them to drive through. They heard a few "What's going on then?" questions from the crowd as they drove past, and one person even tried to run alongside the car as it rolled on. Burton very skilfully swerved to avoid him and, looking in his rear-view mirror, saw the officer drag him back outside the entrance and redo the tape again.

The officer repositioned his helmet which had veered off to one side during the scuffle and stood his ground, positioning himself once again with his back to the tape. The two detectives continued on, tyres crunching on the gravelled driveway, until they parked up behind one of the stationary vehicles that still had its flashing lights on, although nobody was inside it.

'Dispatch didn't say exactly what it was for, did they?' Burton turned off the ignition, thinking that there was already a lot of police activity going on here. Whatever it was that had happened here, it couldn't have just done so as the station had already positioned a constable on duty at the roadside.

'Well, judging by the coroner's van parked up over there,' Fielding said, nodding over in its direction, 'there's certainly been a death. But I'd have thought that it would be quite a common occurrence in a care home. Must be something questionable about it.'

Quickly gathering up what they needed to take inside with them, they made their way up the small flight of stone steps, past the wheelchair ramp and in through the open front door.

There was already a lot of activity in the reception area. Three police officers, none of whom Fielding recognised, were taking statements from a group of carers. One of them looked as if she'd already been crying for quite some time as her eyes were red-rimmed and she had a ball of scrunched up tissue paper right up against her nose. Another carer, a very tall, youngish-looking man dressed in a white polo shirt and a pair of pale green casual trousers, was also being questioned, and although not in the same emotional state as his co-worker, he looked shaken and shocked by what was going on. He was twisting and tugging at the lanyard around his neck so hard, it looked as if he was going to strangle himself with it.

'Oh, I thought you two had already signed off for the evening,' they heard a voice say from behind them. Turning, they found Detective Chief Inspector Elizabeth Ambleton making her way over to them.

'So did we. What's going on, boss?' Burton asked, voicing both his and Fielding's thoughts. 'Seems a bit more than a common or garden old person's death.'

'Well, it is a death,' she informed them, 'and it's an old person, but there's something not quite right about it. The home's doctor was called in to certify the death of one of the residents this evening, but he thought it best to get us in after what he found. The medical examiner is up there now with him, and between them, they think that there's been foul play. Go up and have a look,' she said, looking past them and catching the eye of one of the office staff, indicating that she come over, 'and see what your take on it is.'

Seeing the DCI waving her over, a woman came across to them, dressed in what Fielding thought was a skirt and blouse that were a little too tight for her shape and age. Now, she herself wouldn't even claim to be the sharpest of dressers, but at least she wore clothing that were both age-appropriate and flattering for her. Then she chastised herself for her thoughts. It really wasn't her place to judge someone else's appearance. But being a police officer, she couldn't help but notice people and the way they looked. First impressions, and all that. For that brief moment, she forgot that she wasn't looking at a perp.

Elizabeth Ambleton had been Joe Burton's detective inspector when he was a detective sergeant, but when she had been promoted seven years earlier, he'd been similarly moved up the ranks and Fielding stepped in as his DS. Both his partnerships with the now DCI and Fielding had been good ones. However, not so much could be said about Ambleton's married life – which she kept as far away from her professional one as possible. Burton knew of her daily struggles, but her home life was very much left at home as soon as she walked through her front door in the morning, and kept there for the entirety of her shift.

As directed, both Burton and Fielding followed the member of staff upstairs and they were led to a room at the far end of the corridor on the second floor. The decor was somehow as expected for a care home. Was she being judgemental again? Floral patterned wallpaper above a dado rail halfway down the walls, and almost statutory magnolia paint adorning the lower half. Fielding also noticed a Perspex strip attached to the wall above the skirting boards, most likely to protect the walls from scuff marks caused by residents' Zimmer frames and wheelchair collisions. A practical solution to what must be an everyday hazard in somewhere like this. Her designer elder sister with her apparent trademark plain-coloured minimalism would doubtlessly have tut-tutted at all the home's mismatched floral decor and abundant furniture.

A constable stood outside the open door. Looking beyond him, Burton and Fielding could see two men inside with their backs towards them, who were presumably the doctor and the medical examiner, both bending over an elderly gentleman who was seated in a high, wing-back armchair. They flashed their cards to the constable, who nodded in acknowledgement and gestured for them to go in. Thanking the staff member for her assistance, Fielding watched as she teetered her way back along the corridor on her ridiculously high-heeled shoes. *Maybe suitable for someone in an executive role in a big corporate company in the heart of the city*, Fielding thought, *but certainly not for someone working in the office of a care home on its outskirts. Talk about being overdressed for the wrong occasion!* There she went again, judging someone by their appearance. Second chastisement of the day.

Both heads turned as they entered the room. After the detectives made themselves known and showed their warrant cards, the two doctors, likewise, introduced themselves.

Dr Philip Morton, the care home's doctor, had a thatch of thick white hair and a neatly trimmed matching beard. Looking like a man nearing retirement, his once-smart suit showed signs that it had served him many years in the job. A few creases here and there, a little wear and tear on the pockets, including a loose button on the left cuff, showed he was very comfortable in it despite it being perhaps a size too small for him now. Problems of a sedentary job, the weight begins to pile on after a while. *The man probably wore it every day, slept in it even,* Burton contemplated. Like Fielding, he had over the years developed the skill to make initial judgements about people, and he had no problem with the doctor's appearance. It showed her that he would most likely care more about the welfare of his patients rather than take pride in his own appearance. Even the stethoscope clamped securely around his neck was probably a permanent feature of his, like his suit, and chances were, he forgot it was even there when not in use. In this case, however, it seemed to be redundant as there was now a corpse in front of him with not a great deal of need for it.

Dr Patrick Barnes was a much younger man, in his late thirties or early forties perhaps, and was the on-call medical examiner this evening from the city coroner's office. By stark contrast, Barnes was casually dressed and looked as if he'd just come straight off his sofa, picking up his medical case as he walked out the door. His grey jogging bottoms and tangerine-coloured T-shirt clashed violently with the more reserved elder doctor's garments, showing a generation gap of enormous proportions. Perhaps this was the twenty-first century take on the once obligatory two or three-piece suit – casual rather than formal. The only similarity was the same stethoscope clamped around both their necks, only Dr Barnes seemed to have adopted the habit of taking it off when he'd finished with it – as he did now to speak to the detectives.

Formalities over, they all looked down at the now deceased body of Mr Nathaniel Jackson.

'He was found about an hour ago by one of the carers,' Dr Philip Morton told them, 'and the manager got in touch with me shortly after that.'

'That'll make it about 8.15 then,' Burton said, taking a small A5-size notebook and pen out from his inside jacket pocket. Fielding smiled to herself every time she saw the book, as it reminded her so much of her father who used to always carry one around with him. A policeman's notebook with an elastic strap fixed into the binding to be used as a page marker.

'Yes, but I think he died quite some time before that,' Dr Barnes spoke up, 'judging by what I've seen so far, that is.'

'And what makes you think that?' Fielding asked, looking over towards the corpse. Quickly looking him up and down, she took note of his peculiar appearance. In fact, she'd never seen a corpse dressed in such an odd outfit before.

'I did a few tests on Dr Morton's advice here, and they confirmed that he must have been dead for about two hours before that.'

'Had there been some sort of fancy dress party here today?' Burton asked, looking at the same strange garments which had also caught Fielding's eye.

'Not that I know of,' Dr Morton stated, now showing signs that he was beginning to feel the heat in the deceased's room, as small beads of sweat had begun to trickle down his face and into his beard. The flannel suit couldn't be helping matters either.

'I thought that with Hallowe'en, it was maybe...' Burton trailed off, thinking perhaps that he was being rude to assume that this was a costume and not Nathaniel Jackson's everyday attire. The man may have been an eccentric for all he knew. 'Was this his normal clothing then?' Burton added, not wishing to jump to conclusions.

Dr Morton looked as confused as the rest of them. 'No, certainly not,' he confirmed. 'Mr Jackson has always been such a smart dresser, for a man of his age.'

'How old was he then?' Fielding asked, trying to work it out for herself just by looking at him. But she had to admit that she was having problems trying to guess his age as he could have been anything from late sixties to mid-nineties.

'He was seventy-nine,' the doctor confirmed. 'And quite compos mentis, if that was what you were thinking. He has... had... all his wits about him all right; played scrabble and chess with other residents down in the lounge on a regular basis, and took part in the weekly quiz night... Thursdays, I think... maybe not... sorry, I just can't quite recall which exact night it is...'

'No, that's okay,' Fielding reassured him, cutting in. 'That's not necessary.' She could also feel the heat rising to uncomfortable levels.

'So I really don't understand all of *this*,' Dr Morton stressed, hand outstretched indicating the garments on the body now in front of him.

The man before them now looked far from being a smart dresser or in a good mental state, as the doctor had described him. He was wearing a pair of baggy, old beige corduroy trousers held up with a pair of bright red braces, an oversized white shirt and a navy blue bow tie with white polka dots tied loosely around his neck.

'Looks like a clown,' Fielding murmured, more to herself than anybody else. All he needed was a red nose and an extra-large pair of shoes, and any coulrophobe would be having a meltdown right about now.

'Oh, and there was this,' Barnes said, holding up a playing card. 'It was lying on the floor in front of him.'

'He'd been playing cards?' Fielding asked, looking around, trying to find the rest of the pack.

'No idea,' Morton said. 'That was all there was, I think.'

'Am I free to take him away for examination now, detectives?' Dr Barnes asked, looking keen to remove the deceased away to the mortuary as soon as possible. 'The sooner I get to start the tests, the sooner I can let you know what he died of.'

'So you don't think it's natural causes then?' Burton asked. 'DCI Ambleton said that you thought there might be foul play involved.'

'No,' Barnes confirmed. 'I need to confirm a few things back in the examination room before I can give you a definitive answer. But, from what I've seen, and with Dr Morton's input on his medical history, I don't think it was a natural death.'

2

With the possibility of Mr Jackson's death now being due to unnatural rather than natural causes, the building was placed on lockdown immediately and nobody was allowed to leave for any reason.

The scene of crime forensic team arrived and they quickly set to work under the watchful eye of Dr Barnes, who seemed a little too eager to start work on the corpse. A bit morbid for Fielding's taste, despite all the gruesome deaths she'd seen over the years, but she had to admire someone who threw themselves into their work to that degree. The doctor would just have to wait a little while longer while they got on with dusting and bagging and all the other forensic things they needed to do.

With samples and photographs taken, the SOC team relieved themselves of their protective gloves and white coveralls, and packed up all their belongings into the bags and cases they'd brought with them. As soon as they left, Dr Barnes looked hopefully at Burton, who nodded. He then made a call to his team who were waiting patiently on the driveway in the black van for the go-ahead, and about five minutes afterwards, two gentlemen dressed in formal black suits arrived with a gurney and a body bag, and they began the process of removing Mr Jackson's corpse from the room to the morgue. The crowd on the pavement would be disappointed tonight. Nothing to see, folks, you can all go home now.

Back downstairs, Burton and Fielding informed the DCI of the medical examiner's initial findings and were instructed to conduct interviews with all those present in the home.

'I'm sorry about all of this,' the DCI said. 'I know your team have had a tough few weeks. I can reassign it to someone else in the morning if you'd prefer?'

'No,' Burton said, looking at Fielding then back to the DCI again. 'We're okay on this, boss.'

'Should we rule out the other residents or do you want them questioned too? Fielding added.

DCI Ambleton sighed and rubbed her right temple. She'd obviously had a long day in the office and didn't entirely welcome the prospect of going home to what would inevitably be waiting there for her. 'I suppose we should question everyone. You never know with these old folk, maybe one of them held a grudge or something. Best to question them too... but not tonight. We'll leave that until the morning. Most of them will probably be asleep by now anyway. You might not get much, but we'll cover all our options. Can I leave that up to both of you then?'

The last was more of a statement than a question, but they both nodded. Burton felt sorry for Elizabeth Ambleton. He must make a point in the next few days of having a quiet word with her to see if there was anything he could do to help her situation. He wasn't entirely sure what he could do, if indeed he could do anything at all, but at least it would be good for her to know that somebody was thinking about her during this difficult time. The team had had a bad few weeks, but she was having a bad time at home on a daily basis. They had worked together for a long time, and he knew all the circumstances, so he hoped that she wouldn't mind him talking to her about it. It pained him to see her suffering, so what harm could it do for him to try? And who knows, it may help – even to a small degree.

In total, there were two office staff on duty, the manager and the woman Fielding considered inappropriately dressed, along with ten carers who had started the night shift at 6pm. The twenty residents – or to be more correct, nineteen, now that Mr Jackson was deceased – would have to wait until the morning to be interviewed. Their ages ranged from early seventies right through to late nineties, and both Fielding and Burton surmised that it would take their team most of the next day to undertake the questioning. Under the circumstances, it seemed highly likely that they would be back there themselves sometime during the course of the day.

The manager, a Mr Nigel Pearson, a smartly dressed man in his mid-fifties, suggested that they use the residents' lounge to conduct their interviews, and instructed two of the carers to go ahead and set the room up. The detectives weren't really sure what "setting the room up" entailed as all they really wanted or needed was a private space with three chairs. But when they were shown into the lounge about ten minutes later, the gas fire had been turned on, as had all the lights, and a teapot and coffee pot had been placed on a table along with a jug of milk, a couple of porcelain cups and saucers, and a plateful of bourbon biscuits. Both detectives winced when they saw the drinks options, as another Costa wouldn't have gone amiss at this point.

As the manager handed them a list of all those on duty, they thanked him and asked if everyone could wait outside the lounge until they were each called in in turn.

First in was Lilian Carson, the carer who had found the body.

'Yes, I did think it was rather odd,' the forty-something-year-old woman said, playing nervously with the ID badge on her lanyard when asked about the way in which Mr Jackson had been found. 'He's usually quite the nifty dresser.'

'And you were his usual carer?' Fielding asked her.

'Yes, one of them,' she replied. 'Me and Janis Bowles, who's waiting outside to see you with the others. We do our shifts together. We always work in twos, you see, for lifting and such like.'

'What about visitors?' Fielding continued. 'Did he have any regulars?'

'Well,' began the carer, 'there was only the one regular one that I knew of, his nephew. Came in every few weekends. Said he worked away somewhere during the week... not sure where, though.'

'So the manager would have his address?' Burton chipped in, taking a break from his note-taking.

'I would imagine so, if he's listed on the records as next of kin.'

As everyone present in the home that night came in to give their statements, they didn't learn any more from them than they had done from their first interviewee, Mrs Carson. When asked about the nephew and the next of kin details, manager Nigel Pearson had produced a printed sheet with the information they needed. Quickly scanning it, the detectives saw that the nephew was one Alex Carruthers, whose address was in the city centre.

'Posh part of town,' Burton said to Fielding.

'The carer who found Mr Jackson said that he worked away. Do you have any details about where he can be contacted during the week?' Fielding asked the manager.

'I don't have anything on record about that, but there is a contact telephone number for him,' Pearson confirmed, pointing to it on the piece of paper. Burton added that to his notes, along with the address.

* * *

'I said it was a posh part of town,' Burton remarked, glancing up and down Mason Street when they'd parked up. 'A mate of mine lives in The Village and they are pretty upmarket properties, I can tell you.'

'I bet they're all ultra-modern New York loft-style,' Fielding said flippantly, thinking her sister would have a field day around here, if she hadn't already left her mark on them. Goodness knows how far her portfolio actually extended these days.

'As a matter of fact, they are!' he laughed. 'Not your style then?'

'Let's just say I have a few issues with interior designers and leave it at that.'

'Ah,' he laughed again in a knowingly way, 'sisterly love!'

As it was a weeknight, it was perhaps to be expected that there would be no response from Alex Carruthers's apartment but they still tried his buzzer several times anyway, just as a precaution. As his phone had gone to voicemail, they really needed to find out exactly where he worked as he was all they had to go on at this moment. Even though it was late, maybe one of his neighbours might know the answer, so they tried pressing a few other buzzers and waited for a response, getting an answer on the third attempt.

'Hello?' a woman's voice asked, sounding far away and barely audible. They hoped they hadn't woken her up.

'Good evening,' Burton took the lead. 'We're from Manchester City Police and we're trying to find the whereabouts of a Mr Alex Carruthers. Would you have any information regarding that, ma'am?'

'Alex? Yes, he's my next-door neighbour, but he's usually working away during the week.'

'We're just trying to find out where he may be contacted.' Fielding joined in the conversation, adding, 'May we come in and have a word with you, please?'

'Yes... yes, of course,' the woman said. 'I'll buzz you in. I'm on the second floor, third door on the left.'

When the door buzzed and clicked open, they pushed it to enter and made their way across the spacious entrance foyer to the lift opposite, which was currently on the third floor according to the lit numbers above it. Seeing a flight of stairs just off to the left, Fielding asked, 'Lift or stairs?' To which Burton gave her a withering look. 'Lift it is then.' As she was reaching for the button to call the lift back down to the ground floor, Burton stopped her by saying, 'Just a minute,' and headed off to the row of mailboxes he'd spied on the wall off to the right. If he'd thought about it, he would have spotted Carruthers's one instantly, as the box for apartment number twenty-two had all manner of leaflets and letters sticking out of the flap, which was not unexpected for someone who worked away during the week.

'Nobody to pick his mail up when he's away it seems. He should fill in one of those "no junk mail" requests to the Royal Mail,' Burton said when he rejoined his colleague, leaving the bulging mail where it was. However, if the neighbour was unable to provide them with any information regarding his whereabouts during the week, he would try to slip one of the letters out from the box as it could be a letter from his work, or from somewhere else that could be useful in tracking him down.

Fielding proceeded to press the lift button.

The door to flat number twenty-four was already ajar when they arrived there, and a girl looking younger than her voice sounded on the intercom was waiting for them in a dressing gown firmly folded over herself. 'Come on in,' she said, opening the door wider for them to enter.

'I'm sorry, did we wake you up?' Fielding asked, noticing the way she was dressed and hoping that the answer was no.

'That's okay. I was planning to go soon but got caught up watching one of those stupid reality shows on television!' She laughed ever so gently. 'You said that you wanted to know about Alex; how can I help you?'

'How well do you know him?' Burton said, looking around the apartment. It was very similar to the one his friend had nearby but this one had more homely touches to it, like bright photos on the walls and colourful throws and cushions scattered around the L-shaped leather sofa, which seemed to dominate but not overpower the living space. *Looks nice,* he thought. *Tidy. Tasteful.*

'I don't, not really, only in passing, I suppose,' said the girl.

Burton's notebook came out again. 'Can I just get your name for our records?'

'Oh, yes, of course. It's Monica Williams.'

'So when did you last see him here?' he continued, jotting her name down.

'A couple of weeks ago, on the Saturday. I had a few people around from work in the evening, asked some neighbours, and he dropped in for a drink with his friend.'

'Can you give us a description of him?' Fielding asked.

'Well, I think I can do a bit better than that,' she said, getting up from the sofa and going to get her phone off the sideboard where it lay. Burton found it refreshing to find someone who didn't have their mobile phone held permanently in their hand like most young people did these days. 'I took some photos on the night and I'm sure he was in one of them.' Quickly flicking through her photo file, she eventually stopped and showed them the one she had singled out. 'There he is,' she said, 'second from the right.' The shot showed a group of party-goers in this apartment, glasses raised in a salute, a party popper captured mid-flight in the background, and everyone smiling at the camera. Alex Carruthers looked to be in his mid to late thirties, with dark hair and eyes, and a very winning smile.

She laughed, remembering. 'His friend was really camera-shy as I recall, but as you can see, he was quite the extrovert. Seemed a nice guy; very good-looking.'

Burton asked permission to take a photo of it with the camera on his phone, which he did when she agreed to it.

'Can I ask you where you work?' Even though it wasn't really necessary to their line of enquiry, Burton was curious. It had become a bit of a thing of his, trying to imagine what type of work people they encountered on cases were in. Looking around at her apartment, he had thought maybe she was a designer of some sort, as she seemed to have an eye for stylish furnishings.

He was surprised to hear her say that she was a photographer. 'I have my own business, mainly portraits and wedding photography, you know, that kind of stuff, but I also exhibit my work in the Castlefield Gallery on Hewitt Street. I have an exhibition coming up in the next few weeks if you'd like to come, both of you. You can be my guests on opening night.'

He didn't think he would have time to make it, but he said that that would be nice.

Is Burton flirting? Fielding thought, as it certainly seemed like it to her. Or even, was Ms Monica Williams flirting with him? She must bring it up with him when they left! Flirting, or whatever it was, over and done with, they both thanked Ms Williams for her time and the photograph and took their leave.

'No, of course not!' Burton had retorted when Fielding put the question to him as they were travelling down in the lift. 'Why? Are you jealous?'

'No, of course not!' She gave him the same response that he gave her and they both laughed. It had been a long night, but they both agreed that, before returning back to the station to do the paperwork they needed to do before re-signing off for the night, they should go back to the home to get the staff to officially identify Mr Jackson's nephew now that they had a photo of him. If they couldn't locate him, at least they could circulate his picture via the press or TV to try to find him that way, and a definite ID would set the wheels in motion for that to happen.

There was no constable standing on duty this time, no members of the public trying to get a glimpse of something gruesome, no flashing blue lights on the driveway, and the reception area was not full of staff members confused by, and looking anxious about, the previous strong police presence.

The detectives rang the front doorbell and waited for someone to come and let them in, presuming that there would be office staff in on a twenty-four-hour basis, as well as the carers. After a few moments, they saw the manager through the clear glass panes of the door, making his way towards them. He smiled on seeing them, but looked a little confused as to why they could possibly be back so soon.

'Sorry to bother you again, Mr Pearson,' Burton said as they were being shown in, 'but we'd like you to make an official identification of Mr Jackson's nephew... just for our records.' And with that, he pulled his phone out of his pocket and showed him the photo taken from Monica Williams's phone.

'Who am I looking at?' Pearson asked after scrutinising the picture for a few moments. 'I'm confused.'

Burton and Fielding glanced at one another. 'That's Alex Carruthers right there, isn't it?' Burton asked, pointing a finger at the man Monica Williams had identified as him.

'Why no, detectives, that's not Mr Jackson's nephew. I've never seen this man before in my life.'

3

Sitting across the desk from the detective chief inspector the next morning, after only grabbing a few hours' sleep between them, the overly tired DI Burton and DS Fielding updated her about what had happened after they had seen her at the home the previous evening.

'Well that changes things a bit,' DCI Ambleton said, studying the photo they'd printed out for her of the actual Alex Carruthers. 'Then who the hell is the guy who's been going to the home?'

Even though they knew it wasn't a question specifically directed at them, Burton answered regardless. 'Well, Carruthers has to be thought of as a suspect now, doesn't he? We don't know for certain yet, but the medical examiner last night felt pretty sure that Mr Jackson's death wasn't a natural one.'

'Okay then,' Ambleton continued, still staring at the photograph in front of her. 'The only way forward is to get his picture sent out to the national TV stations and newspapers. If he works away during the week, it looks as if he's much further afield than our local jurisdiction. Gather the team together and update them with what's happening, and make sure the photo gets out to the media for the evening publications and news broadcasts.'

'Okay, gather round,' Burton said, voice raised as he entered the CID squad room with a renewed vigour despite the exhaustion. A sea of eyes looked up in unison from computer screens and the admin staff stopped what they were doing; everyone now fixing their gaze on him and Fielding, who followed in close behind him. 'Where's Simon?' he asked, looking around but not seeing his DC in the office.

'He's just down in records, sir,' DC Jane Francis said, addressing him more formally than usual as the moment seemed to necessitate it. 'He's just putting everything back down there from the last case.'

'Can you go and get him, please?' he asked with a sense of urgency in his voice, which made her spring into action immediately.

'Sure,' she said, looking around at the others in the room before heading off to fetch her colleague from one floor down.

'What's up, boss?' DC Sam Wayman asked him, voicing all their thoughts.

'Let you know when Simon gets back.' And with that everyone fell silent.

DI Burton's team consisted of his detective sergeant, Sally Fielding, and five detective constables – three male, two female. Burton considered that to be a good balance as there were times when same-gender officers were preferred to attend the relatives of the victims rather than a mixed pairing. It was mostly a youngish team. Burton had known and served with them for a few years now and had found them to be the most trustworthy and reliable bunch of colleagues he had ever had the pleasure of working with. Fielding was his most trusted sidekick. Like Batman and Robin, Laurel and Hardy, Morecambe and Wise, even Hall and Oates... you couldn't have one without the other, and that was Joe Burton and Sally Fielding.

He pulled down the projector screen until it completely covered the evidence board and stood waiting for DC Banks's return from records, resuming when his team was complete.

'As you know, we've had a few hard weeks, and I'm very grateful to you for giving up your free time and holidays that you've had booked in during this.' He looked around the room at all of them, then paused. They sensed a 'but' coming. 'But,' he continued, 'DS Fielding and I were called out to a care home in Middleton last night, just as we were heading off shift, to attend to a dead body.'

'That's hardly unexpected though, sir, is it? They must have deaths in there all the time?' DC Phillipa Preston spoke up.

'Maybe not,' Burton continued, 'but the attending doctor and medical examiner who were already on the scene didn't think so. They seemed to consider there was some kind of foul play.'

'In what way?' DC Jane Francis asked.

'Unknown as yet, but we're hoping to get confirmation of that today from the city morgue office. Plus,' he continued, 'there were other circumstances which made it look questionable. Sergeant, could you put the OHP on, please?'

Fielding had been standing beside the overhead projector while Burton was talking, and now on his instruction, started it up. Burton stood to one side as the photo of Alex Carruthers popped up on the screen.

'We're anxious to find out the whereabouts of this man,' Burton continued. 'Alex Carruthers is known to be the nephew of Nathaniel Jackson, the man who died in the care home, and also his next of kin according to their records. This photograph was given to us by his neighbour. He apparently works away during the week, coming home at weekends, so we need to get this circulated to the media as soon as possible. Wayman, I need you to get to work on this one. It needs to go national as we've no idea where in the country the nephew works...'

Banks interrupted, 'What if he works abroad, sir?'

Burton had already thought of that, but said, 'We'll try national first and hope that we can get a result from that.' He turned back to the young DC. 'As I was saying, Wayman, get on to the national press and TV channels. I want his face all over the newspapers and television by this evening.'

'Yes, boss,' he said, adding, 'that's going to be a big job, though, to contact every one of them before this evening.'

Burton considered it. Realising the sheer size of the project and the length of time that it would take, he assigned another officer to join Wayman. 'All right. Summers, can you give him a hand, please.' He thought for a moment and went on, 'DC Banks and Francis, I need you to go to the home and interview all of the residents, see what they have to say about Mr Jackson. Ask if they saw or heard anything out of the ordinary. You might not get much, but try nevertheless. Oh, and try to get an accurate description from the staff of the man who's been coming in saying he's the nephew. Take one of the sketch artists with you.'

'And,' Fielding added, 'ask if anyone knows why he was dressed in what looks like a clown outfit.' With that, the photo projected from the OHP changed from that of Alex Carruthers to one of the deceased in his odd garments.

'Hallowe'en... Bonfire Night? Was there a fancy dress party in the home?' Francis offered, possibly seeing a link to the time of year it was.

'Don't think a man fast approaching his eighties would be doing much dressing up somehow.' Burton nipped that idea in the bud, although it had crossed both his and Fielding's mind when they first saw the way in which he was dressed. 'However,' he added, fully answering Francis's question, not wanting it to look as if he'd quickly dismissed her theory, 'we did check with the staff, and no, there was no fancy dress party or anything remotely like that taking place. It's more likely that he was dressed in this way by whoever killed him, although at this point in time, I have absolutely no idea what that reason could possibly be.'

4

DCs Banks and Francis gathered together what they needed to conduct the interviews at the care home – laptop, voice recorder, a couple of notebooks, one for each of them, oh, and pens – a police officer still needed to be the proud owner of a pen in this day and age – and began to make their way out.

They didn't make it to the door before Burton saw them out of the corner of his eye and called over, 'When you're there,' he said, 'could you also show the residents the clothing Mr Jackson was wearing? I believe we now have individual photos of each article, and we wouldn't want to scare the life out of them by showing a picture of his dead body, would we? See if they recognise any of it. Maybe one of the items he was wearing could be theirs? Anything at all. Thanks.'

And with that they said, 'Yes, boss,' in unison and exited the room, anticipating a long day ahead.

Detective Constables Wayman and Summers also anticipated a long day ahead. Knowing time was against them, they quickly settled down to the task in hand by collating all the telephone numbers of the major newspapers and TV news stations. Then, contacting each in turn, they emailed across Alex Carruthers's photograph. They finally finished at one-thirty, well ahead of the deadline they'd given themselves of two o'clock.

Shortly after they'd finished and Burton was complimenting them on their outstanding efforts, Fielding's phone rang in her back trouser pocket. She glanced at the screen; she was a bit dubious about answering withheld numbers at the best of times on her personal mobile, but curious as to who was calling her, she slid the green 'accept' button across and put the phone to her ear.

'Hello, Detective Sergeant Sally Fielding.'

'Well, hello stranger!' an unfamiliar woman's voice said.

Fielding didn't recognise the voice of the person now speaking, but the woman seemed to know exactly who she was. 'I'm sorry,' she began, 'but I don't...'

'That's okay!' the unknown person interrupted, laughing as she said it. 'I didn't expect you to remember. After all, it has been well over ten years since we last saw one another. It's Claire... Claire Rawlins... we were at school together, well just the last two years really. Remember?'

On hearing the name, recognition set in. 'Claire,' Fielding said in surprise, 'yes of course I remember. How on earth did you find me after all this time?'

'I got your details from Dr Barnes the medical examiner. Thought I recognised the name when I saw it on the card you gave him. You're using your middle name now, I see?'

'The medical examiner?' Despite now knowing exactly who her caller was, Fielding was confused as to how the Dr Barnes she'd seen in the care home could possibly know an old school friend of hers, who she hadn't seen since before she went off to police college. 'How do you know Dr Barnes?' she asked.

'I'm in Manchester, working in the coroner's office; doing a secondment down here from the north east. How uncanny is that?

First job I'm working on and I meet up with an old friend. Who'd have thought it!'

'Yes,' Fielding agreed. 'Who would have thought it?'

'Anyway, the reason why I've officially called you is,' Claire continued, getting back on track, 'not to simply have a chinwag with a long-lost school mate. It's to let you know that the tests Dr Barnes did last night are back from the lab and he'd like you and your partner – is it Burton? – to come down and discuss them with both of you. I told him that I'd ring you and give you a surprise!'

'I appreciate that, Claire,' Fielding thanked her. 'The detective inspector and I will come straight down. And,' she added, remembering what Rawlins had asked her earlier, 'in answer to your question, yes, I'm now using my middle name!'

* * *

'Tannin poisoning?' Burton asked, looking across at Fielding. 'A gradual or large dose of it?'

They were sitting in Dr Barnes's private office in the coroner's office within the Royal Exchange Building on Cross Street.

Claire Rawlins had been sitting waiting for them at reception, and got up when they arrived. Fielding was glad she had, because she had to confess she wouldn't have recognised Claire Rawlins after all that time. After a brief greeting and introduction to her DI, Fielding and Burton were taken through to the medical examiner's office on the second floor. Now they were sitting across the table from both of them.

'Well, it looks like both,' Barnes had to admit. 'When I checked Mr Jackson, I saw that he had a fair amount of abdominal swelling and a yellowing of the whites of his eyes – all symptoms of hepatic necrosis.'

'Which is?' Burton asked, unfamiliar with the name.

'Liver failure,' Claire said, offering her medical knowledge.

Fielding could have never imagined her to be the type of person to go into medicine, let alone end up working in a coroner's office with all the ensuing gore. As she recalled, she was the one girl in school who fainted every time she saw a spot of blood, so picturing her up to her elbows in the stuff was difficult.

'But what made you think that it was other than natural causes?' Fielding asked Barnes.

'Well, Dr Morton and I were discussing Jackson's medical history just before you came into his room yesterday evening, and it seems that there was no history of problems with his liver. Hepatic necrosis can also be caused by HIV medication, but as Mr Jackson was not receiving any of those medications, it seems fair to assume that this was neither natural nor accidental.'

'So he was poisoned then?' Burton was jotting everything down in his notebook. 'And you say both gradual and large doses of tannin had been administered?'

'I took samples of his hair,' Dr Barnes went on to say, explaining the science behind his conclusion, 'and they showed that he had been receiving small doses of it for the past few weeks. Then it looks like he had a massive dose on the day of his death.'

'So how would this be administered then?' More jotting down in Burton's notebook.

'I think it fair to assume by injection. Little at first, so as to not look suspicious, then a very large injection on the day.'

'So do you think that this was done by one of the members of staff, or Dr Morton even?' Fielding had learned over the years not to trust anyone, especially in a case of murder, so the home's own doctor couldn't be ruled out as a suspect from their enquiries.

'Well that's a possibility, I suppose,' Dr Barnes contemplated, 'but that's not for me to say. He certainly wasn't holding anything back with regard to Jackson's medical history. It could even be one of his regular visitors if this was something that had been planned over a long period of time. The man was diabetic, so any needle marks on the body would be seen as sites of injection and nothing more thought of it. Can I just say,' he added, 'as this is now a case of murder, that I've never heard of anyone being deliberately poisoned with tannin before. Surely if someone was going to kill by injection, then the easiest way would be by giving them an overdose of insulin. Very deadly to non-diabetics as well as diabetics, and untraceable in the body after a short while. Why then bother to use tannin, especially when it will be found? It's certainly an obscure one.'

'In that case, it looks as if the tannin has some sort of significance, like the playing card. Mr Jackson only had one visitor, his nephew, and we're trying to find him right now as a person of interest.' Burton paused for a second or two before asking, 'And what did you make of his clothing?' Hoping that perhaps the ME could throw some light on that aspect of the case as well.

'Now that one beats me too,' Barnes confessed. 'They're definitely not his as they're not his size, in fact they're all different sizes. But perhaps they belong to someone else in the home? Either way, it doesn't seem to make a great deal of sense. Why would he put the clothes on himself? Or why would someone else dress him like that?'

'By the way,' Barnes continued, 'did you manage to get any prints from the card found at the scene?'

'The SOCOs found a partial print on it,' Burton told him, 'but as it's so small, they're saying it will be difficult to trace.'

'We must meet up sometime,' Claire had said to Fielding when they were all together in the lift heading back down to reception. She handed her a card with her mobile number on it. 'I'm only here for a short while, staying with a friend. We should get a drink one evening.'

'I'd like that.' Fielding slipped the business card into her warrant card holder and promised that she would get in touch.

'If it wasn't the nephew visiting Jackson in the home,' Fielding said when she and Burton were seated in the car and driving back to headquarters, 'then whoever was impersonating him could have been giving him the poison.'

'Seems feasible to me,' Burton replied, keeping his eyes on the road, 'but to what end?'

'I've no idea,' Fielding admitted. 'But he seemed to know a lot about Jackson's medical history, knew about him being diabetic, which would have made the administration of it a lot easier. We should go through the staff statements again and see if anything stands out, now that we know we're investigating a murder. In reality, anybody there in the care home could have given him it, including the nephew.'

After a pause, Burton turned to his partner and said, 'Did I detect that you didn't seem too happy to be seeing your old school friend Claire Rawlins again?'

'Well, you always were a good detective!' she laughed. 'To be honest, the last two years at school weren't the happiest. As you know, my dad died and my mother and I just sort of drifted apart after that, when she knew that I wanted to follow in his footsteps and join the force. She'd said the force had killed him and said it would kill me too, and we just sort of stopped speaking after that. My elder sister wasn't all that helpful either, saying that I should go out and get myself what she called a "real job". I don't know how she dared...' her voice trailed off. Even after fifteen plus years, the memory of her father's death still weighed heavily on her mind.

'And Claire?' he asked.

'Claire was all right, really. Moved to my area from further up north for the last two years when I was doing A-levels. We kind of hit it off, and she seemed to understand what I was going through. Made a point of befriending me, as I recall. Couldn't stand the sight of blood, though, which is why I'm very surprised by the choice of career she made!'

'And now she's back in your life again.'

'But only temporarily it seems. Didn't she say she was only down here for a few weeks?'

'So, will you be going for that drink then?' He knew that, like himself, Fielding was a loner up to a point. Like him, she'd been in a relationship which had turned sour over time. It was probably why they'd hit it off so well from the start. Something in common between them. He also knew that when a chance came to see an old friend and catch up, that chance should be taken.

'What are you now, my keeper?' She laughed and he joined her. 'Yes, maybe I will,' she said at last, adding, 'just to shut you up!'

* * *

There was silence in the squad room when Fielding and Burton returned in a more serious frame of mind and announced the fact that they now had a murder on their hands. They both knew what that would mean to everyone, especially coming hot on the heels of the one they'd literally just solved. Nature of the job, Burton had told them, but he knew that they were already aware of that fact. The only thing was, none of them had expected a murder enquiry again so quickly after the last one.

However, luck was on their side in one respect. After Alex Carruthers's face had been all over the front pages of all the nation's evening newspapers, and on all the main news channels at 6pm, the police received the call they'd been hoping for. Alex Carruthers rang them at 6.45pm.

5

'I haven't seen my uncle... well, my great-uncle as he really is... for almost two months now.' Alex Carruthers explained over the telephone.

'So you've no idea who could have been going to the care home to see him, saying that they were you, then?' DI Burton asked him, sensing that, despite all their efforts to find the man, it looked as if it had all come to nothing.

'Not at all,' Carruthers replied. 'Uncle Nate knew that I'd be working away for a few months; he had my number to call me if he needed to, as did the home.'

'Yes, we got your number from the manager and left a voicemail on your mobile for you to call us.'

'I haven't received any calls, detective. Sounds like they've given you the wrong number.'

'Does it end in 465?' Burton asked, double-checking the number in his notebook, becoming a little concerned, and mostly irritated by the fact that the nephew, or rather, great-nephew, seemed to be so detached from the reality of his relative's death.

'No, that's not my number.'

Exasperated, Burton decided to end the call, asking Carruthers to come into the station first thing on Saturday when he arrived back in Manchester. But before signing off, he asked where exactly it was that Alex worked during the week.

'I'm working up in Newcastle at the moment,' he told him. 'The company I work for has just opened a branch up here and I'm helping to set-up their computer systems and training staff to use the new programmes.'

As perhaps to be expected, Alex Carruthers's photograph, plastered all over the media the previous evening, had initiated a flood of calls to the station from both newspaper and television companies alike. They all wanted to know why there was such an urgency to locate the man, and all wanted to get the scoop on a potential story ahead of the rest. There was big money in news, especially for the reporters who managed to get the story first.

What bothered DI Burton now was the fact that the care home staff had provided the sketch artist with a face quite different to that of the deceased's great-nephew.

Sitting at his desk trying to finish a sandwich that he'd quickly grabbed from the station canteen, Burton looked at the well-drawn face now looking back at him from the open file on his office desk.

'Who are you?' he said, staring at the picture and hoping for an answer, knowing that none would be forthcoming. Although it was definitely not the face of the somewhat detached Alex Carruthers, he looked about the same age as him and he could see how anyone giving him a fleeting glance at the home could have easily mistaken him for the real great-nephew. The hairline was different, and designer-stubble had been added to the sketch, but there wasn't that much of a difference really. There was no reason at all why he wouldn't have been let in if he'd said he was Carruthers.

The knock on the door pulled him back to reality. 'Come in!' he shouted, and DS Fielding popped her head around the corner of it.

'We've got a problem,' she said, looking as if someone had just kicked her in the teeth. 'There's been another death.'

'At the home?' he asked, rising from his desk and grabbing his jacket from the hook on the back of the door. The rest of his sandwich would just have to wait. Pity, it wasn't that bad either, which was something of a miracle for the station canteen.

'No,' she said, leading the way along the corridor. 'But another team of detectives have alerted us to it; say they've found something at the scene similar to what we found in Jackson's room.'

'Did they say what?'

'No,' Fielding replied. 'But said we should get over there pretty quickly, though.'

* * *

Foxfield Road Allotments were just north of Manchester Airport, and by the time Burton and Fielding pulled up in his car, the lane leading down to the scene of crime had already been cordoned off with the blue and white police barrier tape which they'd now seen a bit too much of in the past two days. A feeling of déjà vu set in when they saw a solitary constable posted beside it. All the scene lacked was a crowd of people around him. Doubtlessly, that would follow as soon as the word got about.

'How on earth can there be any similarity between this and the home?' Burton said to his partner after they'd alighted from the car and looked around them. This was desolate by comparison to the bustling care home, and one had nothing remotely in common with the other.

'Down the lane, sir. About a hundred yards,' the constable said to them, lifting the barrier for them to duck under. As instructed, they ducked and followed the muddy dirt track lane past hedgerows and an assortment of what looked like improvised fences, while at the same time trying to dodge the pools of mud and dirty water following the previous night's heavy rainfall.

Burton could feel his feet becoming damper the further they

went along, and made a mental note to himself to always carry a pair of wellingtons in the boot of his car in future. Fielding looked as if she was dancing, skipping over each puddle as she came to it. *I bet she doesn't have wet feet,* Burton thought, watching her continue along in her own rhythmic way. She definitely had a pattern going to avoid them.

Soon they could see a group of people ahead of them. The SOC team in their familiar white coveralls were already on the allotment, bending over and examining anything they thought may be of interest, and another uniformed constable was talking to two non-uniformed people, a man and a woman, who Burton presumed were the detectives who had contacted their office.

'Detective Sergeant Fielding?' One of the non-uniformed officers approached them, hand outstretched in Fielding's direction. 'We spoke on the telephone, I'm Detective Sergeant Montgomery from the Salford division, and this is Detective Constable Allenson.' She indicated her partner.

Fielding in turn introduced them to DI Joe Burton, and with formalities over, Montgomery led them to where the murder victim was. 'The man who has the allotment next to this one found him when he came down here about an hour ago. We've already taken him home as he was in a bit of a shock by the time we got here; knew the old boy well it seems, and they've had adjoining allotments for the past three years. The deceased's name was Jacob Stephenson,' he said, nodding over to where the SOC team were gathered and busily at work. 'He lived locally, just down the road from here. Can you give up a bit of space, please?' The latter remark was directed to the forensic team, who stopped what they were doing and immediately pulled back.

Mr Stephenson was sitting in front of his spacious shed, halfway down his allotment, on a foldaway picnic chair. A tin cup lay on its side just out of reach of the man's dangling hand. He looked of retirement age, wearing a checked shirt and jeans under a waxed jacket, with a pair of muddy green wellington boots completing his outdoor appearance. His head was as far back as it could go, and his face had taken on a swollen and purplish hue. As the detectives moved in to get a closer look, they could now see that his cheeks were bulging, as if something was filling out the insides of his mouth.

'SOC have already taken a look inside, and his mouth is full of sweets.' Montgomery offered him a pair of nitrile gloves, which he took from her and put on.

'Sweets?' Burton repeated, gently parting the man's lips while gesturing for Fielding to come over and see for herself. She peered in to get a better look. It was certainly a bewildering sight; they'd never come across such an unusual case of asphyxiation before, where the victim had had their mouth stuffed full with multi-coloured candy sweets to choke them. If indeed the scene was as it seemed, and had not been staged to look that way.

'Did the person on the neighbouring allotment say that Mr Jacobson was always here at about this time?' Burton asked, trying to ascertain if this was indeed the place of death.

'Yes,' Montgomery affirmed. 'Always here between eleven and two, apparently. Regardless of the weather. The neighbour can vouch for that. Said you could set the clock by him.'

'So it looks as if he was killed here,' Burton said out loud what he was thinking. He stood up from the body and looked around. It was a desolate spot, ideal for gardeners who wanted to get away from it all, and ideal for anyone wanting to commit a murder. 'So, whoever killed him probably knew his movements, and the fact that this seems to be a very quiet spot and they wouldn't be disturbed.'

'It certainly looks that way,' Montgomery agreed with him.

'You said you found something else here that we might be interested in?' he reminded her.

'We found this on the ground beside the body,' she said, holding up a poly bag with a playing card in it. Burton and Fielding exchanged glances, each knowing what the other was thinking and what that disclosure meant. 'We understand that you found something similar beside the dead body at the care home.'

They had. But that had been the joker. This one was the jack of spades. And it now looked as if the two deaths were related, and committed by the same person.

6

'But it doesn't make any sense,' Wayman said when Burton and Fielding had returned to the station and had gathered the team around to inform them of what had just happened. 'What could the connection be between Mr Jackson and Mr Stephenson, other than the fact they are both elderly men?'

'It's the playing cards that I don't understand,' Banks said. 'Unless...' a sudden thought hit him, 'the joker playing card was beside Mr Jackson in the home, wasn't it? And the jack of spades left next to Mr Stephenson who was found at the allotment? Joker... spade... just thinking. Was Jackson supposed to be dressed up to look like the comic book character of the joker, and did Stephenson have the spade left beside him because he was a gardener?'

'It's a possibility,' Fielding said. 'Maybe they did know one another, and the playing card signifies gambling, perhaps? Did they play cards together? Did they both owe money to somebody and were killed for it? Leaving a card, and a different one at that, seems to signify something.'

DC Phillipa Preston offered her take on things. 'Maybe there was some sort of older person's underground whist drive, and the victims owed money to another member of the club?' Along with Fielding's idea, and Wayman's seemingly odd suggestion, this had actually started them thinking about a money connection. 'Well, let's face it,' she continued when seeing a spark of interest in the other team members, 'we've had very odd reasons for someone committing murder, haven't we?'

'Well, it could be I suppose,' Fielding said. 'As you say, we've had far stranger. Plus, if there's money involved, then I'm sure that there may even be some sort of connection to the city's more criminal element. The cards certainly seem to be important.'

At that point, Burton's office door opened. A telephone call had temporarily dragged him away from the discussions. 'No connection to one another,' he announced, with more than a hint of despondency. 'Just come off the phone with DS Montgomery. She's spoken to Mr Stephenson's widow and she'd never heard of a Mr Nathaniel Jackson, or the care home in Middleton.'

As he was listening to the theories the team had come up with during his absence, DCI Ambleton appeared in the doorway, looking as if a great weight was hanging over her. 'I'm sorry, everyone,' and she really did look as if it was grieving her to say it, 'but I've had to call a meeting with the press and media in the main conference room this afternoon. This has come directly from the commissioner's office, not from me, before I get the full blame for this. The media were all over this before when we were looking for Carruthers, but even more so now, now that we have a second death. I don't know who's leaked this so soon or where they got the information from but they seem to know about the playing cards that were found at both scenes.'

Fielding looked around the room at the DCs and the other administrative staff present, unable to imagine that any of them would be irresponsible enough to jeopardise their investigation to that degree; but she also recognised the fact that money talked – and any newspaper or journalist would pay a pretty penny for a titbit of information that would give them the edge in the game of printing exclusive news first before their rivals. Still, it was far more likely that somebody from the care home had contacted the press rather than a member of her own team. Or so she hoped.

'We've got a couple of theories about that, boss,' Burton said, dreading the prospect of having to go up against the media so soon after the last case they'd just closed. He'd faced the newspapers and television reporters a few times in the past month and they'd never said anything kind about the police during this time, despite all the team's time, their hard efforts and emotional involvement in the homeless man's case. Not even an apology in the end when they'd solved it; and it wasn't by sheer luck either, but rather by their procedural detective work and the entire team's dedication and devotion to the job. *Journalists – scum of the earth*, he thought to himself.

Listening to their ideas, the DCI thought anything to be possible at this stage, but felt certain that the cards were a definite link. Otherwise, why leave them? Yes, they were important to the killer somehow – but for what reason? 'Now, I know that I don't have to tell you this, Burton, but don't go telling them more than they need to know about this. I know just how much you hate these conferences. So do I. But I'll be sitting there alongside you, and if you need help, I'm right there. Just say that we are investigating two unrelated deaths, claim ignorance on the playing cards if they come up – which they probably will if they already know about them – and show them the sketch artist's drawing of the phoney nephew, saying it's someone we are looking for to help us with our enquiries. And...' she added, before exiting through the door, 'for God's sake don't even mention the possibility of a serial killer. That's the last thing we want the media getting their grubby hands on right now.'

Burton's relationship with the press was something he didn't care to think about. The DCI had said to him once, 'Better a bad relation-ship than no relationship with them.' But he completely disagreed with that statement. He couldn't count the number of times he and the press had locked horns over the years, and the last thing he wanted was to go up against them again today. They may well have their uses in that they could convey messages out to the public – like putting Alex Carruthers's photo all over the media – but in his mind, that was all they were good for. He had learned from experience that, if they didn't have or weren't provided with a story, then they would simply go ahead and make one up for themselves, which was bad news for everybody – especially the police. But perhaps he was being a bit cruel. He didn't doubt that, out there somewhere, there were some good reporters – it was just that he'd never once in his life actually met one.

Preparing himself mentally for the verbal assault, DI Joe Burton closed his eyes and took a few deep breaths as he waited outside the conference room with his DCI. From the safe position on this side of the door, he listened to the noise from within. He could picture the scene he was about to venture into: camera flashes, television crews, journalists all vying for the best position near the front, all waiting to launch a barrage of questions and give him the third degree about what was looking to the team to be the beginning of a serial killer investigation. That's what comes from being the senior investigating officer on a case, having to face the inevitable media wolves at the door. The DCI gave him a quick glance and nodded for them to go in. *Here we go*, he thought. *Like lambs to the slaughter.*

As expected, the room erupted when they entered and they took their seats at the table which had been set-up to face the hordes. And there were hordes – about ninety or a hundred faces confronted them, mouths all moving at the same time, with either hands in the air already eager to ask a question or pen in hand, hovering over a notebook, eagerly waiting to take down whatever was said. He saw

BBC, ITV and SKY news cameras pointed at the two of them, all set-up and ready to go. Burton couldn't hear himself think, such was the level of noise in there, and he could feel the start of a headache moving its way across his forehead from his left temple to the right. That was all he needed on top of everything else.

'All right, all right, keep the noise down, everyone. We're here for a press conference, not to hold some sort of battle re-enactment!' Sounding every bit like a head teacher in an unruly school assembly, DCI Ambleton's voice boomed into the microphone on the table in front of her, causing a brief burst of very high-pitched feedback on the last word. A few of the reporters covered their ears at the sound of it.

Burton smiled inwardly to himself; he'd enjoyed that.

When she thought that the noise had subsided enough, she spoke again. 'Detective Inspector Burton will answer any of your questions today but please bear in mind that this is an ongoing criminal investigation, so there is only so much that we can give you. Okay, let's begin, and you can start your cameras now.' She looked towards the TV crews as she said it.

Of course, nobody listened to a word she had said, and questions came flying fast and furiously from all parts of the room about every single aspect of the two deaths. He heard Ambleton sigh beside him. Even without turning to look at her, he could picture her rolling her eyes right now – and that brought another smile to his face. Hopefully nobody caught that on camera, as he could imagine the headlines accompanying that one. At least it took the pressure off him for a few seconds before the cross-questioning began. All the usual questions came flying one after the other, and Burton stayed calm throughout, strongly fighting back the urge to give them the most ridiculous answers he could. 'How long will the enquiry take place?' and 'Do you have any suspects?' being just two of the standard run-of-the-mill questions to which he would have loved to have replied to by saying, 'How long is a piece of string?' and 'Of course we have, we've already made an arrest.' But he behaved himself for his boss. He'd promised her that he would.

Then the big one: 'Paul Johnson, *Manchester Evening News*. So, do you think that there's a link between the two deaths, detective inspector, or are they unrelated?'

Actually, Burton was surprised it had taken so long. It was the question he had been dreading, and the one the DCI had warned him about, so he was aware that he had to respond to it with extreme caution. The room fell silent as all eyes fell on him, everyone eagerly awaiting his reply. None more so than the detective chief inspector.

Taking a breath, DI Burton answered that question in the only way he thought possible under the circumstances. 'We are treating both deaths as suspicious, but do not know if they are linked at this moment in time.'

'But could they be?' Paul Johnson continued to push for an answer.

Pushy little sod, Burton thought, but he wasn't going to give in that easily. 'You'll know as soon as we do, Mr Johnson – you all will,' he said, looking around and directing his gaze from the reporter to the rest of the people in the room.

'Okay, that's all we can tell you today,' DCI Ambleton said, rising from her chair, sensing that her DI was nearing the end of his tolerance with them. She indicated for Burton to do likewise despite the expected protestations from the crowd before them. 'As the detective inspector said, we will keep you updated with any further progress in this matter. Thank you all for coming.' And with that, Ambleton and Burton turned to leave despite demands for them to stay, and made their way back to the safety of the far side of the conference room door.

'Well done, Joe,' Ambleton said when they walked through the door and it had closed behind them. 'You held it together well.'

'Just.' He laughed, eager to go off and grab himself a good cup of coffee, and relieved that it was now all over. 'I hate them, all of them, they just get my back up every time.'

'I know they do,' she agreed. 'Me too, but sadly they are a necessary evil, and we just have to grin and bear it and play along with it. Like I said,' she gave him a gentle pat on the back, 'you did well.'

7

Parting company with Ambleton at the lift, and promising to keep her updated every step of the way, Burton made his way back to the incident room. As he pushed open the door, DC Francis shouted, 'Sir,' and waved a hand in the air to catch his attention. Seeing it, he walked over to her desk.

'We've just had a call come through about a break-in in Altrincham. The next-door neighbour saw something going on in the empty property and her husband went out to investigate, and got himself a head injury for his trouble. He's currently in hospital in a critical condition.'

Fortunately, this time it wasn't anything linked to the 'Playing Card Killer', as the press had so kindly called the murderer. They hadn't actually referred to him as a serial killer yet, but that would doubtlessly come in due course. Fortunate in that respect, but unfortunate for the poor victim of the break-in. As Burton sent DCs Banks and Francis out to speak to the injured man's wife, he brought Fielding up to speed about the press conference.

'I think we should go and question the man who has the adjoining allotment to Mr Stephenson's, and also speak to the widow,' he said, grabbing a bottle of water from the mini fridge and almost downing it in one go. 'When I spoke to DS Montgomery from the crime scene before going into the conference, she said that she'd been to the dead man's house afterwards, but she didn't have the sketch of the man claiming to be Mr Jackson's nephew. It's a long shot I know, but the widow or the friend may recognise him from somewhere, or even know him, even if they think there's no connection with Jackson and the home. Perhaps the man had been to see Mr Stephenson at his allotment?'

Fielding nodded. 'It might very well be a long shot, but it's all we have to go on at this moment. I'll ring DS Montgomery and get their addresses from her.'

'Mr Stephenson's widow has gone to stay with her son for a while,' Montgomery told her when she rang. 'I'll text his address over to you, along with the friend's address from the adjoining allotment.'

'Before we go,' Burton said to Fielding, 'can you get in touch with Northumbria Police and get someone to go out and have a word with the manager of the company where Alex Carruthers works during the week. Have him confirm Carruthers was actually there the past few days. He's the only suspect we have at the moment, but if he was up there in the north east, then he couldn't have been down here in Manchester now, could he? Which leaves us having to try even harder to find that person posing as Jackson's nephew. They'll understand your accent and you theirs; they'll not have a clue what I'm saying.'

Fielding gave him a withering look and he laughed, even though he didn't feel up to laughing at that moment.

* * *

Peter Cousins lived just a short distance from the allotments, and looked as if he was still suffering from the shock of finding his friend dead when he opened the front door to Burton and Fielding.

'We're sorry to disturb you at this difficult time, sir,' Burton had said after they had been invited in and were sitting down in his front room. He would have put Cousins at either late sixties or early seventies, judging by his first impressions of him. Although these days, he had to admit, it was becoming more difficult to determine a person's exact age as older people – especially in the age bracket he'd guessed Cousins to be in – were looking a lot younger than they used to. It was clear to look at him that here was a man who enjoyed the outdoor life. His ruddy complexion was a testament to that, but at this precise moment in time, the ruddiness had given way to a pale, washed out look which frequently followed shock. He was probably itching to get back to his allotment right now, desperate to in fact, but Burton felt that what he'd found there earlier would hamper his keenness to get back there any time soon.

'I know I've got to go back there to get everything sorted out for the winter coming along,' Cousins said, looking wistfully out through the window, 'but don't see how I can face it for a while yet, considering, you know, finding him like that.'

'Well you don't have to, Mr Cousins,' Fielding tried to console him, but sensed that it wasn't helping; he looked too far gone for that. 'That's understandable, and I'm sure one of your friends can come along and help you with that.' She could see a tear trickle down his cheek from his watery eyes.

'Jacob was a good friend. We spent many hours down the allotment, me and him...' As his voice trailed off, Burton and Fielding glanced at one another, sensing the pain of his friend's death tearing him apart and feeling utterly incapable of helping him.

'Do you live here on your own, Mr Cousins?' Burton asked him, understanding Fielding's look of concern regarding the elderly man and how he was reacting to what had happened.

Mr Cousins nodded. 'Missus died a couple of years back. Was just me, Jacob and the allotment after that... and now he's gone too...' His voice faded away again.

'Any relatives who could come and stay with you, or you go to them?'

'I'll be all right,' he said, wiping a tear away. 'Got to be, haven't I?'

'Can you think of anyone who would want to harm him?'

Mr Cousins looked at Burton with an expression that looked like a combination of shock and disgust. 'Hurt Jacob? No, nobody, absolutely not. You couldn't want for a nicer man, he was the salt of the earth... salt of the earth.'

It was clear that he wouldn't be able to help them, so Burton decided to call it a day and leave the man in peace. But he did think that it might be a good idea to contact social services once they'd left, just to make sure that somebody could look in on him, check that he was okay. The two detectives got up to leave, but before going, Burton asked the one main question that they'd come to ask. 'Have you ever seen either of these men before, sir?' And brought out a copy of the sketch artist's drawing of the man they urgently needed to find now that they'd discovered he wasn't Alex Carruthers, along with a photo of Carruthers himself.

Cousins took the images from him and went in search of his reading glasses, which he eventually found in the kitchen on the workbench beside the cooker. As he scrutinised the faces on them for quite some time, both Burton and Fielding felt that there was no recognition in the man's eyes. However, he finally declared, 'Yes, I think I've seen him down the allotment before,' pointing at the sketch artist's drawing. They felt as if their luck had changed for the better, only to be let down promptly again when he added, 'but I've no idea what his name was or where he'd come from. Looked official though, was dressed decently enough. This one,' he said pointing to Carruthers, 'I've never seen him before.'

They thanked him before leaving, then headed back to the car. As they now had good reason to believe that their unknown man may have met with Jacob Stephenson at some time, they hoped that the victim's widow may be able to help them. Perhaps her husband had talked to her about him, maybe she'd even seen him? With that in mind, they decided to pay her a visit at her son's house where she was now staying. They knew that it didn't necessarily follow that she would know, but it was another line of questioning they had to pursue, and couldn't afford not to.

One thing Peter Cousins had said interested them, though. He'd said that John Doe – they'd decided to now refer to him as John Doe, considering that they had no idea of his identity and couldn't keep calling him 'him', 'the man', or 'the faux nephew' – looked official. Perhaps he was from the council? As all the allotments on this site were rented on an annual basis through them, it was something they would follow up if Stephenson's widow couldn't be of any help to them.

* * *

Jacob Stephenson's son lived in a peaceful but expensive leafy suburban street in north Salford.

'Wonder what he does for a living?' Fielding speculated as they pulled up on the road beside the driveway to a very large, detached house.

'Must pay a great deal judging by the look of it,' Burton said, looking the extensive premises up and down. The house, or perhaps a more fitting description of it would be a mansion, was quite the contrast to his two-bedroomed apartment just outside Manchester's city centre. This must have at least four, maybe five bedrooms over its two floors, and a very generously-sized double garage just off to the side of it. They had already called ahead to say they were coming, so were expected. As they walked up the path towards the front door, they could see movement through the blinds of the large window off to the left of it, which was presumably the living room, and then the front door opened for them. A smartly-dressed man in his fifties greeted them, introducing himself as Jacob Stephenson's son, Joshua, and invited them into his home.

'I'm not sure what my mother can tell you, detectives,' he said, leading Burton and Fielding through the hallway and into the spacious living room area, 'but I'd appreciate it if you didn't question her too much. Our doctor came in earlier and prescribed her some very strong sedatives and she's already taken them, so I'm unsure how well she will respond to your questions.'

Two women were seated on the L-shaped leather sofa and the younger of the two rose as they entered. 'My wife, Lisa,' Mr Stephenson Junior said, introducing her to them, 'and this is my mother.'

Jacob Stephenson's widow looked very frail and remained seated. She looked up at them but the detectives could see by the look in her eyes that she had already had enough sedation for the day – maybe even for the next few days too.

'We're so sorry to have to bother you all, but we would like to show your mother a sketch of a couple of people who may have been known to your father.' Fielding directed her question to the son who remained standing.

'As you can see, I'm not sure what you will be able to get from her but please do so if it will help you.'

Burton sat down on the sofa next to the widow and took the sketch and photograph out of his inside jacket pocket. 'Mrs Stephenson,' he began, and the woman turned slowly to face him. 'Do you recognise these men at all?'

It came at perhaps no surprise that she was unresponsive to his question. Burton glanced at Fielding and knew she was thinking the same as him: they were not going to get any further with this line of enquiry, as neither the son or his wife recognised the images. The only thing they had to go on now was to contact the local council to see if John Doe was from their allotments department as Peter

Cousins had suggested. They'd get a couple of the detective constables to go and check it out when they got back to the station.

But when he checked the time, Burton realised that it was too late now to have John Doe's photograph circulated around the council offices today. 'Get on the phone to the station and tell Banks and Wayman to get down to the council first thing in the morning. The more people about, the more chance we have of getting a lead – if there even is one. Allotments come under parks, playgrounds and open spaces, as I recall. Tell them that too.'

As instructed, Fielding rang the station as they were driving along. The rain had started again and was beating against the windscreen with a vengeance, and Burton turned his wipers up to their maximum speed. Deep in thought about the events of the past two days and concentrating on the busy road ahead, he hardly heard a word Fielding was saying. Rush hour was well and truly under way. Everyone was eager to get back to their loved ones and spend the night in the warmth and comfort of their own homes as this storm looked to have settled in for the night. Heavy rain had been forecast for around five, and here it was, lashing it down and probably contributing to people going a lot slower on the roads than they normally did at this time of the evening. His car now seemed to be stuck, right slap bang in the middle of it, and he'd been forced to slow down to almost a snail's pace.

It wasn't until Fielding had finished her call and he heard her say his name that he snapped out of his thoughts. When he took his eyes off the road and glanced at Fielding, her face was ashen.

'What's wrong?' he asked. He hadn't seen such a shocked look on his partner's face for quite some time.

'Turn around, we need to get to the general hospital fast. Right now. Simon Banks has been injured and he's in surgery.'

8

Although Burton was full of questions about how this could have happened, he didn't speak again until they pulled up outside North Manchester General Hospital on Delaunays Road in Crumpsall, just over three miles north of the city centre.

Screeching to a halt, Burton parked up in a yellow chevron restricted area just outside accident and emergency, usually reserved for ambulances and other emergency vehicles. Hurriedly, he rummaged around in the driver's side pocket for his 'police on duty' sign to put on the car's dashboard. He found it tucked away behind a letter he'd forgotten to post the previous day. Cursing, he slapped it down onto the dash behind the steering wheel just as a paramedic alighted from the ambulance next to them and started to make his way over. He saw the sign go up on the car window, stopped in his tracks and pulled back. Burton had seen him begin to approach and shouted, 'I'll move it as soon as I can,' as he and Fielding sprinted past him. He also spied a group of people huddled together at the next entrance down. *Reporters*, he thought, seeing a camera crew setting up their equipment right beside them, but they managed to get into the building before they'd even noticed them arrive.

Flashing their warrant cards to the queue already formed at reception, they asked the receptionist the whereabouts of their detective constable. She informed them that he was still in surgery, but if they wished, they could wait with his other colleagues who were already at the second floor visitors' area.

When they exited the lift on the second floor, they saw Jane Francis and Phillipa Preston sitting with a few other people on the blue chairs at the far end of the corridor. Jane had her head bent right down on her chest, and Phillipa was sitting next to her with her arm around her shoulders, trying her best to console her. It didn't seem to be working. On seeing Burton and Fielding approach, Preston stood up and walked towards them, informing them that the other two DCs were on their way but held up in traffic. Burton could believe it, judging by what they'd just driven through.

'Does the DCI know?' Burton asked, making his way over to Jane, who'd raised her head on hearing his voice. She looked pale and in shock, and he could see blood all over the front of her blouse and trousers.

'Yes,' Preston said, 'and she's on her way too.'

'We saw the press outside when we came in; they're on the ball as ever,' Fielding said to Preston.

'They weren't about when we arrived. News travels fast, it seems,' Preston told her.

'Yes, bad news always travels quickly,' Fielding agreed with her.

'Sir,' Preston added, 'these are Simon's parents, and his wife and daughter,' indicating the elderly man and woman and the younger woman with a child who were sitting a couple of seats away from them. He had not met Simon's wife and daughter before, but he recognised them from the photographs of them proudly displayed on his desk; none of which, he had to admit, did them any justice.

At forty-two, Simon Banks was the oldest member of the team and had been married to his stunning Polish wife, Agnieszka, for only three years. They'd met while he was visiting her country for a friend's stag party, and the once confirmed bachelor had fallen head over heels for her at first sight. His beautiful daughter, Hanna, aged two, was the apple of his eye and he was as devoted a husband and father as anyone could be. This made the situation seem even worse to Burton. Simon Banks had waited a long time to find the woman of his dreams, and his life was now hanging in the balance. For him to lose his life now would be an unspeakable tragedy for everyone.

'Is he going to be okay?' Mr Banks senior asked him, standing and shaking Burton's hand when he held it out to him.

Burton thought that to be an odd question as he wasn't a doctor, but the older man's faith in his son's boss touched Burton. 'I don't know anything yet, sir, I'm sorry,' he had to admit. 'We just got the news when we were heading back to the station. We don't even know how it happened.'

'The young girl there,' Simon's father said, indicating Jane, 'said that they'd been investigating a break-in when somebody hit Simon with a weapon...' His voice trailed off and his wife reached up to grasp his hand, and he sat down again. Burton placed a consoling hand on his shoulder.

'Jane,' Burton said, crouching down in front of her, 'I need to know just what happened... if you're up to telling me.' Fielding sat down on the seat beside her and reached for her hand to hold. It was damp from the soggy tissues she was holding.

She looked up at him with red-rimmed eyes, the colour of Simon Banks's blood on her clothing. 'We went to Altrincham, like you said, after that man was injured, to talk to his wife.' She inhaled deeply. 'She said she'd been in the kitchen and happened to see a torch light coming from next door. She knew that the house was empty and up for sale, so she told her husband to go out and take a look. They thought that it was unlikely that somebody was being shown around it in the dark, so the man went out to see what was going on. The next thing the wife knew was that her husband was calling out for her and when he got in through the back door, he collapsed on the floor. Looked like he had been hit on the head with something, and he's now in hospital – this one as a matter of fact.'

Jane paused as if to organise her thoughts. 'As we were looking around the outside of the property – Simon was around the back and I was at the front – I heard Simon cry out and heard someone running away, and then I found him... on the ground. I rang for an ambulance... and...' Jane stopped. 'There was so much blood coming out of his head and his side. I just rang 999 and kept my hand pressed on the side wound. It was just gushing...' she took a quick look to her left and stopped as she saw Simon's parents were listening to what she was saying. They didn't need to hear all that.

Burton, realising why she'd stopped, took her free hand and squeezed it tightly. 'You did good,' he told her. 'You've probably saved Simon's life.' Jane knew that he was saying that as much to Banks's parents as he was to her.

'I don't know, sir,' she whispered so that the parents couldn't hear, 'they say he's pretty badly hurt.'

At which point DC Sam Wayman appeared out of the lift and headed their way. He looked tired and rubbed his eyes as he walked. Life was hectic for him outside of work as well as in it. The twenty-six-year-old Cornishman was married with three children, two girls and a boy, all under the age of six. His colleagues joked that he came into work each day to escape from the chaos of his very hectic home life, and to get a bit of peace and quiet. Today was not one of those days.

'The DCI is outside with Summers,' he told Burton, 'and she's talking to the press as we speak. They pounced on us when they saw us coming in. Couldn't break away from them. I think she's asked him to stay with her for moral support. They're coming up when they are through.'

Burton thought that she wouldn't have needed much support as she could be quite a formidable character when she put her mind to it.

They must have sat for about an hour before anyone came out to see them, during which time Ambleton and Summers came and went, asking to be kept up-to-date with Simon's progress every step of the way. Eventually, two doctors, who looked like they had just come straight from theatre as they were dressed in green medical scrubs and had their face masks pulled down beneath their chins, made a point of coming out to speak to them all.

'I'm Mr Williamson and this is Mr Waterstone,' the taller of the two surgeons introduced themselves to the group.

Everyone stood up, including Simon Banks's family.

'We've successfully operated on Simon and he is now in recovery,' Williamson said. 'He sustained a pretty bad head injury and a side wound which fortunately didn't go near to or damage any of his major organs, but he's now doing well and is going to be fine. We need to keep him in for a while, though. He just needs rest and time to fully recover.'

'Can we go in and see him?' Simon's wife asked, her daughter clinging to her as she spoke.

To which the surgeon replied, 'Yes, but only you and one other person at the moment, please,' looking around at the police officers, adding, 'I'm sure you'll all understand that he needs time to get well again and everyone going in at once will just be too much for him at the moment. Perhaps one or two of you could come back tomorrow to see him?' At which point, Burton and the team took their leave, while Simon's wife and his mother followed the two surgeons to his room. His father and his daughter followed on behind, saying that they would wait outside his room, and that his father would go in later.

* * *

As they couldn't stay and see their colleague, Burton decided to call it a night then. By the time they all left the hospital, all the reporters, TV crew, Summers and the detective chief inspector had gone. There was no doubt that this would now be all over the evening newspapers and television news reports. Saying goodnight to DCs Francis, Preston and Wayman, Burton watched them all get into Preston's car and drive away. He had told them all to go home, and everything could be written up in the morning rather than going back to the station and doing it tonight. He'd drive Fielding home himself, then, hopefully, settle down for the night and try to get his head around all of this.

They'd hardly got themselves settled in the car and moved off when the call came through from dispatch, directing them to an address just past the care home in Middleton.

'Now what?' Burton said. The last couple of days had been non-stop. They'd hardly had time to turn around and it now seemed like they were being bombarded from every conceivable angle. They had a baffling murder to solve, they had no idea who their John Doe was, they didn't know what to think of Alex Carruthers, and now one of their own had been injured and hospitalised. What else could possibly go wrong?

A lot, it seemed, for as they were drawing up at the address that they'd been given, both their phones pinged to notify a message had been delivered to them.

'Why can't people just ring?' he said mostly to himself as his and Fielding's message read exactly the same thing:

```
Need 2 c u @ morgue Barnes.
```

'And what the hell is this? We're all supposed to be professionals here, not kids texting one another just for the fun of it. Bloody hell!' Burton was past tired. Fielding knew it, but was reluctant at this moment to point that fact out to him. For one thing, he most likely knew it too; and secondly, the way he seemed to be at the moment, he would very likely bite her head off. Joe Burton had, in normal circumstances, the most passive personality she knew. But on the very rare occasions that he exploded, she knew that nobody was safe, not even her. No, she certainly wasn't going to say a thing. No way.

Burton was about to tell her to ring both Francis and Preston, to get them to go down to see Dr Barnes straight away, but then realised he'd given them and the other DCs the night off and he felt that he couldn't contact them again under the circumstances. 'Text him back if that's how he wants to play it,' he told Fielding. 'Tell him what's happened this evening and say that we'll be down in the morning, first thing.' Fielding did as she was told.

'Oh Jesus, what's this?' Burton exclaimed as they exited the car and saw arc lights coming from the back garden of the address they'd been given. 'Please don't say we have another one? I wish these dispatchers would tell us exactly what we're going to when they contact us.'

The constable on duty at the gate lifted the crime scene tape up for them and they ducked underneath it. The feeling of déjà vu set in. As they followed the path to the front of the house, it then veered off to the right and led them to the gate of the garden's six-foot-plus fence. Lifting the latch, they pushed it forward. It opened to reveal a big, well-stocked garden with a white tent already set-up near the centre of it, men and women kitted out in the mandatory white Tyvek suits dotted around the lawn and a couple of plain-clothed police officers hovering around them. Burton and Fielding made their way over to the tent, a sense of dread coming over them the closer they got, feeling that whatever lay inside may well be connected to the other two murders.

Seeing them coming, two male officers met them halfway and introduced themselves as Detective Constables McKenzie and Walton.

'We weren't expecting anybody else, sir,' McKenzie said, a little puzzled by the arrival of two additional detectives on the scene. 'Our DS and DI said we could handle this one ourselves.' Adding, when he realised he was addressing two detectives who outranked them both, 'Of course, we're very grateful, sir, considering the nature of it.'

'We got a call from dispatch,' Fielding felt the need to explain, as everyone seemed confused, including them. 'We weren't told that anybody else was here either. Doesn't look like it's just happened, though,' she continued, knowing that to set things up to the degree they were now set-up, took some time to organise.

'No,' DC Walton told her, 'we've been here for about an hour now, haven't we?' The last question being directed towards his colleague, who nodded in agreement.

'Okay, let's get inside then,' Burton urged, not really wanting to stand around making polite conversation on a night that was turning colder by the second.

The two detective constables led them into the tent, but not before DC McKenzie turned towards them and said, 'Brace yourselves, it's not a pretty sight.'

It never is, Burton thought, and they weren't wrong. Kitted up in a white suit, the ME was still bending over the body of an older woman, if her clothing was anything to go by. It looked as if her head had been completely squashed by a very heavy object.

Fielding fought back the urge to vomit; she'd never seen a death as violent as this one before – and she'd seen more than a few violent deaths in her relatively short time on the force.

'Oh, hi again,' a familiar voice greeted them, as the ME lifted her protective goggles and positioned them on the top of her head. 'Didn't think I'd be seeing you again so soon.'

How could Claire Rawlins be so upbeat at a time like this? Fielding wondered. Hazard of the job no doubt, detaching yourself so far from the very nature of it that you become impervious to any element of shock. 'No, me neither,' Fielding said, still battling the almost overwhelming nausea.

'I would ask what have we got, but I can clearly see.' Burton looked the body up and down, seemingly unaffected by the sight that was now disturbing Fielding so much. 'I'm assuming it was murder and that she simply didn't fall and bang her head on something while out in the garden?' A somewhat redundant question, and unexpectedly humorous for him, especially under the circumstances.

'Very astute, DI Burton,' Claire Rawlins said. Did Fielding detect a hint of humour in her voice too? 'And you're right, of course. We haven't found the weapon of her death at the scene, but from what I can see of her injury – and it's a pretty severe one, as you can tell – I would say that she's been hit several times with a very heavy object, a large hammer, mallet, club or something of that nature. Definitely wood though, as I've found traces of wooden fragments in her head.'

'What head?' Burton asked, staring down at what was in effect a liquefaction of blood and brains.

'Well, what was the head, detective inspector,' Rawlins replied.

'What do we know about her, Claire?' Fielding asked.

'Dorothy Johnson. Lives here with her sister, Elizabeth – both spinsters, both love gardening – and that's really all we have right now.'

'Did the sister find her like this?' Burton could only imagine what that had been like for the other sibling, seeing your flesh and blood – and lots of blood, at that – dead in such a disturbing manner in her own back garden.

'Yes, she did,' DC Walton joined in the conversation. 'She had a heart attack after she rang 999 and has now been hospitalised.'

'It's definitely the sister then?' Fielding asked.

'Yes, she recognised her clothing,' DC Walton replied, adding, 'thankfully.'

'There's one more thing I think you might be interested in, DI

Burton,' Rawlins said, reaching for a poly bag from the inside of her metal forensic equipment case and holding it up for him to see. It was what he had dreaded seeing and had deliberately not asked if it had been present at the scene, but there it was now, in front of him: another playing card, but this time it was the queen of clubs. This confirmed to him that they were now dealing with a serial killer.

Burton's mind was now on the next press conference.

9

'So what do we have, Joe?' The DCI was now sitting across the desk from Burton, having requested that he come along to her office the next morning.

'A bloody nightmare, that's what we have, boss,' he responded a bit more aggressively than he'd intended, adding, 'sorry,' when he realised how it must have sounded.

'No... I agree with you, this whole thing is becoming a media circus, especially with Simon being attacked as well. They're now pestering the super for more information as we are – in their words, and I quote – "just sitting around waiting for the next murder to happen". Are there no leads at all on the sketch artist's drawing?'

'Not a damned thing, boss. Nobody's seen him, nobody knows him... we've hit a solid brick wall with it. I've got a couple of detectives down at the council offices right now, trying to find out if he's something to do with the parks department, but in all honesty, I'm not hopeful in the least that they will bring anything back with them.' DCI Ambleton could sense the desperation in her DI's voice; she felt as despondent as he did.

'What about the ME? I believe that he texted you last night asking you to go and see him?' Ambleton asked.

'I was going to send a couple of DCs down there yesterday evening when Fielding and I were called to the latest crime scene, but didn't want to bring them out again, especially after what happened yesterday with Simon. So we texted him back to say that it would have to wait until today, and Fielding popped along there this morning. Dr Barnes wanted to tell us that he'd found a small, barely noticeable syringe mark at the base of the neck, which he assumed was to render them unconscious prior to them being killed.'

That only served to add to their problems, but Burton was grateful that Dorothy Johnson had been unconscious before the killer had smashed her skull. That also applied to all the other victims. Although each death was equally horrendous, at least they were not aware of it.

'We've just heard back from SOCO, and they've found a partial print on the second playing cards now,' he added.

'Have they managed to get anything from them?'

'It's only half a thumb print and, apparently, they can't get any sort of identification from it; they'd already told us that about the print on the first card. But what's curious is,' Burton continued, 'the same half thumb print is on the second playing card, in exactly the same position as the first one – bottom left-hand corner. And not just another print but the exact same print, identical in every way, right down to its positioning. And now there's another card, and I'd bet my pension on that being the same print on that one too.'

Ambleton thought for a moment before speaking. 'Sounds like it's been planted there on purpose then. Half a print in exactly the same place. That's not a coincidence – or an accident. That's deliberate. I think whoever has done this, is playing a game with us.'

'I have to agree with you, boss,' Burton said. 'Although I've no idea what this game is.'

'The super has said that perhaps we should enlist the help of a profiler. What's your take on that Burton?'

Burton sighed. He wasn't that keen on psycho-babble, as he

chose to describe it, at the best of times. Every profiler he'd ever had anything to do with always seemed to produce the same standardised idea of the type of person the killer was: white, male, within a certain age group, of above average intelligence, killing for either sexual gratification or power. He felt their clouded judgement hampered police from looking for the real killers, the ones with the most motive, rather than for someone who fit their stereotypical profiles.

'You know my views on them,' he told her.

'Yes, I do,' she said, remembering that they'd had this conversation before. 'That's exactly why I asked you.'

'Well, we've got nothing else. I suppose so, if the super's saying we should get one in.'

'Right, I'll get this organised for you,' Ambleton said, reaching for the telephone. Burton took this as a sign for him to leave. 'Oh, Burton,' she added as he was about to leave the room, 'how did you know to go to the murder scene last night?'

Thinking that a strange question in itself as the DCI knew exactly how the dispatch system worked, he said, 'Fielding and I got the call through from dispatch after we left the hospital last night. Why do you ask?'

'Well, you see, that's the thing,' she said to him, hand over the mouthpiece of the phone, 'dispatch say they have no record of anyone having called you yesterday.'

* * *

'But that's impossible!' Fielding exclaimed when Burton returned to the incident room and told the team what Ambleton had said. 'How can that even be?'

'Sounds like someone has somehow managed to intercept dispatch calls. Easy enough to do, I suppose, if somebody really wanted to do it.' Wayman hardly seemed surprised by what Burton had said. 'Nothing anybody does really surprises me these days,' he went on to say when all eyes turned questioningly on him.

'But that means that the killer has led us along right from the start then.' Fielding still had trouble processing the whole information. 'We were led to the first death at the home by a call from dispatch, or from someone now claiming to have been from dispatch.'

'We've been used as pawns,' Preston commented, echoing all their thoughts.

'We've been used all right.' Burton slammed his fist down hard onto the desk in front of him, making one of the admin staff jump with shock and drop the manila file she was carrying. As Fielding had observed earlier, Burton's usually mild-mannered temperament had been replaced by a new unexpected aggression, but with this case coming so hot on the heels of their previous one, it was perhaps not unexpected that it was leaving its mark on him. It was leaving its mark on all of them. Two explosions in the short space of two days just weren't part of the DI's character.

'The DCI has suggested we get a criminal profiler in, and I've had to say yes. As I left, I think she was trying to get it sorted for us.'

'I know a good profiler,' Phillipa Preston offered. 'And I'm sure she'd be happy to come in and join us… if you like, I can contact her?'

'Well, I think it may already be sorted, but I agree, it would probably be a good idea to get somebody in who knows the team. These psychologists or psychiatrists can be up their own arses sometimes and think they're way above anybody else, not even listening to what we say.'

'She's actually my girlfriend, sir,' Preston felt obliged to say at this point after his perhaps disrespectful outburst.

'Oh, I see,' Burton said, sometimes wishing that he would keep his mouth shut and keep his opinions to himself.

'But I'm not just trying to push her in because we're in a relationship. I happen to think that she's one of the best profilers out there – and we can trust her. She'll listen to what we have to say and won't be going off on her own agenda. She'd be working with us and not against us, sir.'

Burton thought her argument was an acceptable one, and he felt pangs of guilt for calling all profilers and labelling them all with the same tag. He didn't know anybody who actually knew one. They all just seemed to come in and do their own thing in their own annoying way. But that was what he'd grown to believe based on his past experiences with them. 'Okay,' he finally said, 'I'll have a word with Ambleton and get that sorted. In the meantime, Francis get on to the media again, press and TV, and get them to run that photo as a priority by the end of the day – if not sooner. Tell them to say that this person is now wanted in connection with a murder enquiry; that should keep them happy for the time being.'

'Anyone know how Simon is this morning?' Francis asked, and everyone stopped.

'Yes, I rang the hospital this morning,' Burton told them, 'and they say he can have a couple of visitors at a time. If anyone would like to go in during the day, please feel free to do so, just let me know beforehand when you're going. I'll pop in this evening... Fielding, you up to a visit as well?'

She nodded confirmation. 'What about the house break-in? Do you want us to investigate it, or should we ask a couple of the Altrincham officers to go out and take a look? Maybe interview the neighbour's husband while they're at it too?'

Burton pondered while considering. 'Yes, get them to look at the property, find out anything they can about it, and ask them to speak to the wife next door. We can go and see the husband this evening when we go in to see Simon. Francis,' he said, 'I'd like you to come with us this evening as well. I want to ask both you and Simon what you remember about yesterday – absolutely anything at all, no matter how small or insignificant it seems to you. Is that okay?'

Francis confirmed that she'd go with them.

10

One of the best things about having a conservatory was the fact that you could sit in it at any time of the year to relax and enjoy the view of the garden beyond. Having thermal blinds on the windows and roof enabled this year-round comfort, making the extension both cool in the summer and warm in the winter. It was also a good vantage point to watch your pet exercising itself without having to expose yourself to the elements, especially when the uncertainty of the autumn and winter months' weather set in. Such were the thoughts of retired NHS worker, Sandra Matthews, as she sat in the comfort of her glass house in Cleadon, Tyne and Wear, while her pet golden retriever, Sammy, ran enthusiastically around the garden lawn outside. It was a well-tended space, despite the plants and trees looking a little forlorn now that the summer had passed.

She picked up the novel that she'd set aside on the coffee table when she let Sammy out and began reading it again. About five pages into it, she heard her dog begin to bark, slowly at first but then increasing to a more hurried pace. Looking up, she saw him in the top corner of the lawn facing the fence that adjoined the next-door neighbour's garden, barking with a sense of urgency at some unseen thing.

Opening the conservatory door, she called out for him, 'Sammy, come back here, boy,' but he didn't seem to want to stop, and even moved closer to the fence, putting his front paws up onto it and scratching frantically at the wood. Realising that something was bothering him, Sandra slipped on her wellington boots which were beside the door, pulled her cardigan across her and went out to see what all the commotion was about.

'Keep the noise down, Sammy,' she said to him as she got closer, but he still wouldn't stop, and seemed to want to try to climb up the fence now as well. Something was definitely bothering him as he was, by nature, a very placid dog.

There was a small gap in the fencing and Sandra put her face up against it to try and see what he was barking at on the other side. It was then that she realised what he was getting so agitated about, and she wished that she hadn't been so curious about it.

What she saw was her next-door neighbour, Caroline Porter, a youngish woman who she knew very well, lying on her patio. But not just lying on it. One of her planters near the French doors leading to the dining room had had the contents taken out of it and replaced with water, and she was lying face deep in it.

Leaving Sammy where he was, still barking, she ran back into her conservatory and into the kitchen, pulling open the drawer where she kept her neighbour's key with such a force that it almost came out of its runners. Hands shaking, she quickly grabbed hold of the fob it was on and flew through her front door. She knew that time was of the essence here, as Caroline may well have just collapsed and was drowning at this very moment.

Reaching the patio, she lifted the girl's head up from out of the planter but realised as she was doing so that it was already too late. Her neighbour's body was already cold and rigid.

Sandra almost dropped her back in there in shock. The only

thing she could do was to try to lift her up and turn her over onto her back. She knew from all the television detective programmes she watched that she really shouldn't touch or move the body, but she couldn't leave her neighbour with her face down in the water. She would just have to explain that to the police when they came. Knowing that she would have to ring 999, she headed back to her house to call them, but as she was doing so, something floating in the water caught her attention. Although puzzled by it, she left it there and hurried back to her own home.

Northumbria Police responded to the call within ten minutes, by which time Sandra Matthews was beside herself – and her dog wasn't faring too well either. He appeared to be just as traumatised as his owner.

'It was my dog who heard something,' she said when the police and the SOC unit arrived at the scene. 'He started barking at the fence down the bottom of the garden there.' She pointed in its direction.

'But you didn't see or hear anything, Mrs Matthews?' the DC asked her, jotting everything she was saying down in his notebook.

'No, not a thing... oh, and it's Miss Matthews by the way. Like I said, Sammy was the one who did, not me. She was such a nice girl. Who would want to do a thing like that?'

'So you don't think it was an accident then, Mrs... Miss Matthews?' the officer continued.

'No, I don't. I don't think it's an accident when somebody empties a planter, fills it with water and then puts their head in it, do you?'

'No, I don't,' he was forced to agree. 'I have to ask you, though,' he continued, 'why did you move her?'

'I know that I shouldn't have,' Miss Matthews confessed. It was the question she had expected. 'But my first thought that she must have collapsed and fallen in there. I thought that I could pull her out and try CPR; I was a nurse before I retired. But I didn't think that she would already be dead...' her voice trailed off.

11

A fter speaking to the police commissioner and contacting the psychology department at the University of Manchester, DCI Ambleton had been given the okay for profiler Louise Simmons to come along and join the team for the duration of the case. DC Phillipa Preston was, of course, delighted, but she would make sure she kept a highly professional front in her girlfriend's presence.

'Don't worry, Burton,' DCI Ambleton told him when they were both sitting in her office awaiting the arrival of their new addition to the team. 'I've checked her out, and although she's relatively young, she's already proving to be one of the best psychologists in the Manchester area. These newly-qualified psychologists have had access to both old established theories and all the new ones too, and apart from DC Preston's recommendation – and, by the way, Burton, I wouldn't have taken her on because of just that – she has the backing of some of the big bosses in her department.' She paused for a moment. 'You and your team, Joe, are the best I have here, and this is in no way a reflection on your work. No way at all, and I hope you realise that. You and Fielding, and the rest of the team, well, I can't fault any of you on anything. It's just that with the killer leaving a calling card, quite literally... this is something we need a psychologist's advice on. We need their insight on the killer's mental state.'

Although not in total agreement with his superior, Burton knew that they had no other leads they could follow at the moment. Truth of the matter was, the profiler seemed like their only hope.

The phone rang shrilly on the DCI's desk. 'Okay, send her up,' Ambleton said into it and replaced the handset on the receiver, looking in Burton's direction. 'Play nice, Burton,' she added. 'She's all we've got right now.'

Louise Simmons was an extremely attractive young woman. *Anyone failing to notice that fact must be mad*, Burton thought as he looked her over. With her dark auburn hair tied up in a bun, horn-rimmed glasses, smart leather briefcase, off-white shirt with a neat bow at the neck and grey pinstripe suit, she looked every inch the professional.

'I think that you've already been made aware of what we are up against here?' Ambleton said to her, and she nodded. 'We'd really appreciate a psychologist's view on this, as there are no apparent motives or connecting factors in these murders that we can find through normal police investigation.'

'I'll see what I can do for you, chief inspector,' she said.

Yes, very professional, Burton thought.

Back in the incident room, Burton formally introduced his team to the profiler while Ambleton stood in the background looking on. She stood her ground until, introductions over, Louise was shown to a spare desk, took her coat off and began to get down to business. She knew that Burton and his team desperately needed a break on this one and hoped that Simmons would be able to throw some sort of light on the type of person they were looking for.

Happy for now, she headed back to her office with more than she had earlier. The first thing the profiler wanted to do was to see the crime scene photographs and the case notes. Francis was assigned to help her with that.

While she was going through all the information, Fielding took an incoming call from a member of the SOCO team. 'I just wanted you to know, DS Fielding,' the officer began, 'that the print found on the card last night is the same as on the other two.'

Fielding's heart sank; this case was becoming a nightmare of mammoth proportions.

'I've compared all three,' he went on. 'And if you want my professional opinion, I'd say they've all been placed there deliberately. The exact half a thumb print on all three cards in exactly the same position, that's no accident. Unfortunately, as I said before, there's no way in the slightest we can trace it, not even with today's technology.'

Fielding thanked him for all the information he had provided, and ended the call.

At the same time, Burton received a telephone call from a DS Swanson with Northumbria Police. As instructed, one of their uniformed officers had gone out to see the manager of the company Alex Carruthers was working for during the week, and he had confirmed without a shadow of a doubt that he was working there, so Carruthers had not been in Manchester over the last few days. It wasn't what Burton had hoped to hear, but he thanked DS Swanson nevertheless for his help and assistance.

Louise Simmons wasted no time in getting into action. She'd already glanced through the files and photographs and had started to post up the crime scene photos on the cork board. She put up shots of Jackson's body, then Stephenson's, then finally last night's victim, Dorothy Johnson. Underneath each of the three photographs, she added the image of each of the playing cards found at the three crime scenes.

The fingerprint-dusted cards each clearly showed the print, and Fielding could see what the SOCO had meant when he said that they were exact matches – same place, same half-print. Looking at them in this way, all together up on the board side by side, she could see the similarity and the pattern which was emerging.

Simmons took a few steps back from the board and looked it over, eyes darting from one picture to the next. 'This is a very odd one,' she said at last. Burton and the team had already realised that and didn't need anybody else to tell them. 'And you say nobody has come forward regarding the sketch artist's drawing?'

'No, not a thing,' Burton confirmed. 'We've drawn a complete blank with that one. Just the usual attention-seekers and time-wasters coming out of the woodwork.'

'And what about the call you received from dispatch sending you to all three of the murder scenes?'

'I've got a couple of the detectives questioning the dispatch team upstairs right now as we speak.'

Simmons scrutinised the board again. 'Well, I can tell you that you are not dealing with a typical serial killer here. Although, by looking at the cards that were left at the scene, it looks like you are most certainly dealing with the same person. Although what the motive is – other than the obvious one of gambling – I just can't say at the moment.'

Great, Burton thought, *nothing we didn't know already then. How can this possibly help? But give the girl a chance,* he told himself, *if only for Ambleton's sake.* After all, he had promised that he would play nicely.

'What about the people themselves, are they linked in any way?' Simmons asked, looking quickly at the file.

'Apart from them all being elderly and retired, there's little else that we can find,' Burton told her.

'I see that Mr Jackson from the care home is a retired head teacher, albeit he retired over twenty years ago. What about the man from the allotment and the lady last night? What do we have on their line of work?'

'I'll get a couple of the detectives down to both addresses to check this out. Although,' Burton added, recalling Mrs Stephenson senior's physical state when they saw her at her son's mansion, 'it might be wiser for someone to call Mrs Stephenson's son rather than go and see her.'

While Burton was waiting for the DS he'd assigned to find out the relevant information, Louise Simmons talked Fielding and himself through the basics of criminal profiling as it applied to what she had in front of her.

'Usually,' she began, 'a serial killer is someone defined as having murdered three or more people, with the murders taking place over more than a month with some time between each murder. This is where your case differs significantly. For example, all three deaths have taken place in a matter of days; this is not the usual known pattern. There's an urgency to it, a need to get it over and done with very quickly, and this is very important to the killer. Traditionally, and by universally accepted criminal profiling standards, serial killers are white males, late twenties to early thirties, with a higher than usual IQ. But as the murders do not fall into the known standards, I'm quite confused as to who we are actually looking for here.'

She paused and looked from Burton to Fielding. 'I think it might help to find out what all their professions were prior to retirement. If we can find out if they were all in education in some form or another, then that would be a great lead.'

'Why is that then?' Fielding asked, trying to see where Simmons was going with this.

'Well,' Simmons responded, 'at least we would have a good link if that was the case. Usual motives for killing include power, abuse and revenge. Just assuming that education could be the key, then maybe the killer was abused at school perhaps, and is seeking revenge. It's just a thought... if the link was their employment and that employment was in education. There is another option, of course,' Simmons added, till scrutinising the photos on the cork board.

'Which is?' Burton was almost fearful to ask as there was already far too much going on in this case than he cared to think about.

'Well, only one of the victims might have been the intended target.'

Psychologists, off on a tangent again, Burton thought, but just said, 'Go on, explain.'

'I've known that it has happened before in cases of multiple murders. One person is the actual target of the murderer but, in order to cover it up, or to make it more difficult for the police to catch the perpetrator, they kill other random people as well.'

'That's very interesting,' Burton admitted. 'We did think that Alex Carruthers was a prime suspect for his great-uncle's death, but that's just fallen apart as I've just received confirmation that he was working up north at the time the old man died – and also, when the other two murders took place. So it couldn't have been a case of him bumping off the relative for money or whatever the motive may have been, then bumping off a few more just to cover it up.'

Despite Burton's irritation at having to call a psychologist in, he had to confess that she was seeing things from a different viewpoint, ones they hadn't instantly picked up on. The killings seemed to have been non-stop over the last few days, one following hot on the heels of the other, so another person's take on it was more welcome than he'd first cared to admit. Truth was, Louise Simmons coming in was the first positive thing to have happened in the last few days.

'Of course, there's yet another possibility,' Simmons said to him.

'And that is?'

'That Alex Carruthers had an accomplice.'

Burton hadn't seen that one coming. And that made a whole lot of sense.

12

The national and local evening newspapers had a field day when they discovered that there had been another murder, and were up in arms that they hadn't been told about it. Burton didn't feel it was his duty to keep the press updated with every single little thing as it happened, but they apparently didn't agree with his way of thinking, referring to both him and his team as, quote: 'A bunch of incompetents who couldn't catch a killer if he came up to them and confessed.' He wasn't happy with the slight on all their characters, the DCI wasn't happy and, even worse, the detective chief superintendent wasn't happy.

With another press conference on the cards and pencilled in for that very afternoon, Burton wanted something specific to give them, without giving anything away. Following Louise Simmons's theory regarding the victims' previous professions, the investigating DC had finally caught a break in the case and found the connection: Nathaniel Jackson, Jacob Stephenson and Dorothy Johnson had all worked in education in their past. Jackson had been a head teacher, as was already known, Stephenson a janitor and Miss Johnson a school secretary. None of them had worked in the same school, but at least there was now a tangible link between all three.

The playing cards though, now that was still the confusing piece of the puzzle.

'I still think it must be gambling,' Fielding had said, trying to keep Burton's mind off the pending press conference, knowing how much he hated both them and the press.

'But none of them gambled; that's been confirmed,' Burton told her.

'Secret gamblers then.' Fielding was determined that this was the only possible thing that the cards could signify. *What else could it be?*

Burton sighed the sigh of a man beyond tired. 'In that case,' he rubbed his temples, 'we need to question not only the neighbours and relatives, but also the friends of the victims as well.' This line of questioning could go on forever, though. What the hell was he going to say to the press?

'I've been doing some research on that, sir,' Preston chirped up, overhearing their conversation. 'On the whole question of the cards, that is.'

'Go on,' Burton said, taking an interest. Any sort of lead or theory would be better than none at all at this moment.

'Well,' she began, consulting the sheet of paper in front of her. 'Fortune telling. In India, the symbols on cards have astrological aspects. Each of the four suits have a different meaning too. A heart represents spring and the element of fire, and it is supposed to allude to our childhood. The club represents summer with earth as its element, with emphasis on education and the irresponsibility of youth. A diamond signifies autumn and the element of air, representing the time we are growing and developing our responsibilities. Finally, the spade represents winter and old age, when a person learns wisdom. The element for this is water. The only thing I can get from all this that has a bearing on our cases is the mention to education and childhood, and the irresponsibility of youth. Perhaps the link is related to something that happened when all three were in education. But I know that this had already been suggested.'

'That does seem to be a possibility, but it all seems a bit contrived and personal to the killer rather than him, or indeed her, trying to tell us something. Although, didn't Simmons say that, generally, serial killers are supposed to have a high IQ? Don't they also say all serial killers ultimately want to be caught? If that were the case, then maybe they shouldn't be so vague when leaving their clues. And the astrology thing, that seems to imply a more ritual aspect to the killings, doesn't it?' Burton surmised.

'Then there was this,' Preston continued. 'I've tracked down two cases within the last two decades linking playing cards to a crime scene – which is more appropriate to what's going on here. From 1999 to 2005, there was a series of five murders in Japan. All deaths were different, apart from the fact that the killer left a playing card at the scene of the crime, with a word written on it with the victim's own blood. There were little clues at the scene, apart from the cards, and someone was eventually arrested but released as there was no real evidence to convict him. The case eventually went cold and has remained unsolved to this day. Then in 2003, in Spain, Spanish police named a serial killer of four victims the "Playing Card Assassin", due to the fact playing cards were left at the bloodstained scene in Madrid. The police said they were looking for a "psychopath… a strong, dark and agile young man". However, in this instance, the playing cards were tarot cards rather than the usual standard playing cards, ranging from the ace of cups upward – the cup cards indicating emotional fulfilment.'

Burton now felt even more confused than he did before, but the two things that stuck out in his mind from these instances were the link to education… and to emotion. The profiler had suggested it, and now Preston had brought both in in an abstract way from the general information dug up from the Internet on playing cards. And as for the motives – as the two sets of murderers who had deposited playing cards for the purpose best known to themselves had never been captured, there was nothing to be learned as to why they'd committed the crimes, so this was something that would never be answered. *Trust the killers never to have been caught*, Burton thought. He would loved to have heard the reasoning behind it. If nothing else, it had given him food for thought.

* * *

'Now remember, Burton,' the DCI told him before he was due to go into the press conference, 'like I said before, don't give them too much, just give them enough. I'm not going to be in there with you this time, so you'll be going it alone.'

'But we haven't really got anything we can give them, boss. Again, there's been no response with the drawing of John Doe – and I don't think there's going to be now. All we have is another murder, and a gruesome one at that. That's probably all they're here for, truth be told...'

'Now, Joe...' Ambleton scolded him.

'Well,' he continued, ignoring her, 'we all know that they're all in it for the money – first one to get their story or photo back to their editor, that's all that matters to that lot in there.'

'They can be of help sometimes, as long as we feed them the right information,' the DCI persisted. 'And in this case, I think we can tell them that we've found a link between all three victims. Perhaps that will get the people each of the victims have worked with, thinking. Maybe they remember somebody each have tangled with in the past. Somebody with a grudge perhaps? There must be a common denominator in this somewhere, especially as they've all worked in the same profession. A pupil who has attended the same schools they worked in maybe? It happens – families can travel around and some children end up in a handful of schools during their time in education.'

Burton sighed again. 'I know you are right,' he admitted, 'but it's just that I hate the lot of those press scumbags.'

DCI Ambleton patted him firmly on the back. 'I know you hate them, but they don't have to be the enemy you know, as long as you keep your hatred at the back of your mind. Just feed them a few titbits of information and let them print it in the hope that we can get something back from them in return. You're not the only one with the weight of the world on your shoulders, you know.' A friendly smile.

Burton suddenly felt guilty for his now regular outburst at the press. He knew she and her husband were struggling with their son Charlie's problems; in fact, he didn't know how she could come to work every day in such a high-profile job and still function properly under the circumstances.

'Okay, in you go.' The DCI almost pushed him up to the door before leaving for the meeting she should have already been in five minutes ago.

Of course, nothing went to DCI Ambleton's plan. Burton's hackles were raised almost immediately by an infuriating little ferret of a man from a Scottish newspaper who insisted that the Manchester Police Force was the worst possible police force in the country – did he include Scotland in that, Burton pondered? – and were clueless as to how to go about finding a suspect and making an arrest. Burton wanted to go up to him right now and knock the smirk off his face in front of all present. The journalist started them all off with questions and insults all coming at him at the same time until he thought that his head was going to burst open right there and then with the pressure of it.

'Will you all shut up!' he yelled at the top of his voice, even though he realised that he was being filmed by all the nation's TV news channels and this would be all over the evening news before the end of the day. Ambleton would be having a fit right now if she knew. He could see the headlines in his mind's eye: Manchester police officer explodes on camera. Scottish press reporter to blame. Scottish press reporter murdered by inept investigating officer.

The silence was deafening after his outburst; you could have heard a pin drop, as the saying goes. *Just give them enough. Just give them enough.* Ambleton's words went round and round in his head. He also thought about that cold six-pack of beer in his fridge, and how he was probably going to demolish it all when he got home tonight. 'Let's have some order then so we can carry on with this,' he said firmly into the microphone and, much to his great surprise, they complied. Having momentarily found his inner calm, he continued.

'Thank you for coming, ladies and gentlemen of the press. I can confirm that we now have three victims of what appears to us to be same killer.' He held his hands up in the air for silence as the voice level began to rise in the room. 'If I may continue.' Giving them a moment or two to settle down. 'We know that all three people were in education before retiring, so we are looking for someone who must have come into contact with all three at some time in their careers – someone who has worked with them or someone who attended their schools as a pupil, or someone who has a reason to have grievance against all three. We are also releasing photographs of the three victims, which were taken during their working lives, in the hope that people will recognise them from those days. So, if anyone has any information regarding them, or can think of anything that would help us with our enquiries, can we ask them to contact the telephone number on the table in front of me.' Burton referred to the 0800 number which had been printed out on a banner and attached to the table beneath the microphones. 'We still wish to contact the person in the sketch artist's drawing, so if anyone thinks that it might be them, or if anyone knows this person or thinks they may know this person, please let us know so that we can eliminate them from our enquiries.'

'Has a criminal profiler been assigned to your department, DI Burton?' a voice called out from the crowd.

On the ball, this lot, Burton thought to himself – and not the Scotsman this time. 'Yes,' he confirmed, feeling it redundant to deny it as they evidently knew already anyway. 'We are being assisted by a profiler from the University of Manchester who has been seconded to the unit for the duration of the enquiry.'

'Can we have their name?' another person called out.

Knowing that Louise Simmons's life would be made a misery if he let them have her name, he simply said, 'I'm not prepared to give that out at this time.' Despite their obvious protestations, Burton felt that he'd given them enough for the day and duly closed the conference. He'd half expected Ambleton to be waiting for him in his office when he got back to give him grief, despite the thought that he'd handled himself admirably after the first hiccup of that abominable Scottish man, but he hadn't anticipated what happened next.

13

A part from Ambleton, Fielding and Simmons were already in his room when he got there. 'Look, boss,' he began, anticipating the worst, but she cut him short.

'I heard what happened, but I don't blame you, Burton. No, it's not about that. We've just had a call from Northumbria Police, up in the north east. They'd like one of us to go up there as they had a couple of murders around two months ago which bear a striking similarity to ours. They didn't say in what way specifically, but they think it warrants investigation. Fielding here,' Ambleton turned to Burton's second-in-command, 'has volunteered to go as it's basically her neck of the woods and she knows her way around Newcastle and the surrounding area. She's also asked if an ME can go along with her. If there's such a similarity, she thinks it a good idea to take Claire Rawlins who is already working on the case. Thought that she could look at the forensic evidence they have, see how that compares. Plus, Claire knows the area well, as that's where she's from and works too.'

'Well, if it's okay with you, boss,' Burton said, although sorry to lose his DS for a couple of days.

'Fielding has spoken to Rawlins and she's happy to join her, and she has permission to go from the coroner's office, so the two of them are going up to Newcastle on the evening flight. I wish Northumbria Police had been more specific about details, or sent down any relevant information, but they seem to think that we should see what they have in person.'

Ambleton stayed on after Fielding and Simmons had left, and had a few words of wisdom for her DI. 'Look, Burton, give yourself a night off. Let the press work on what you've given them today. You and your team have been hard at it non-stop over the past few weeks. The homeless man case was one of the hardest I've ever seen in all my years in the force and every single one of you worked so hard to catch the killer. You've no idea how proud I am of you, all of you in fact, and the sooner we catch this vicious bastard, the sooner you can all get the time off you all deserve. It will be interesting to see what Newcastle has to say. Let Fielding do her job and hopefully, it could just be what we need to crack this case wide open.'

'Will do, boss,' he told her. 'I'll be happy to go home, but not before I go to see Simon in the hospital and find out exactly what happened yesterday. I'd asked Fielding to come along as well, and Francis, but if Fielding is now heading off up north, it will just be me and Francis going.'

As Burton and Francis drove off to the hospital to see the recuperating Detective Constable Banks, all he could think about was that six-pack chilling in his fridge that would have to wait a while longer.

* * *

Detective Constable Simon Banks was looking a lot better than when Jane Francis last saw him. He was sitting propped up in bed in a hospital gown in a private side room off the main ward and was joking with the nurse who was attending him.

'Hey, Simon,' Burton said as he and Francis entered the room, 'great to see you keeping your spirits up.'

'Yes, he is,' the nurse laughed, who, going by her name tag, was called Mary, 'but I think he'll be with us for a few more weeks yet.'

'Quite right too,' Burton agreed with her, adding on a lighter note, 'I see he's keeping you amused then?'

'He's quite the comedian this one,' Nurse Mary told him.

Really? thought Burton, who would never have pictured his Simon Banks as a stand-up comic, he was always such a serious young man at the station. This was a side of him he hadn't seen before. But, come to think of it, the poor lad hadn't been hospitalised in the line of duty before, so maybe he was just grateful to be alive. That in itself could change a person's personality. He remembered one of his friends from back in London, who'd always been a bit of a joker and a lover of life until one day he was shot while on duty. It had been touch-and-go for him for a while and he'd come through it okay, but he'd never seemed the same person again after that. Everybody on the force likes to think that they are invincible to some degree, but Burton had assumed that this friend of his had seen his own mortality and it had left him with a different outlook on life. The whole experience had changed him, that was for certain.

'Just a quick little injection and then he's all yours,' Mary said, preparing the biggest syringe Burton had ever seen in his life.

'We'll leave,' Burton said, already starting to move towards the door.

'No need,' Mary told him. 'I'll be pulling the curtains around the bed so you two can stay put.'

As she concealed their colleague behind the drapes, Burton cringed at the thought of the 'little injection', as Nurse Mary had put it, being inserted into Banks. If that was a small one then he'd hate to see a big one.

When the curtains were drawn back, Simon Banks seemed completely unfazed by it all.

He even had a smile on his face. *Morphine*, thought Burton, *got to love it.*

After making sure that Simon was comfortable and wasn't wanting for anything, his nurse bid her farewell and took her medicine trolley with her as she left the room to leave him alone with his visitors, but not before a final warning of, 'You'd better be quick, though. That injection will knock him for six in a few minutes.'

Seeing that time was now of the essence, Burton pulled a couple of seats closer to the bed for himself and his DC and got down to the business of asking both of them to give him a full account of what had happened.

'We answered the call that came through asking for officers to go to a property in Altrincham, where a man had been injured fending off an intruder who had broken into the house next door. By the time we got there, the man, Mr Markham, had already been taken to hospital. This one, so I hear, and there were a couple of uniforms waiting there until we arrived,' Banks told him.

Francis noticed that he seemed to be a little out of breath despite his momentary high spirits, so she continued with the account. 'We spoke to the wife. She was very shaken up but told us that she had been standing in the kitchen doing the dishes and saw what she thought to be a torchlight shining through the window in the house next door. There's only a low fence between the houses at that point and her kitchen looks straight into next-door's kitchen. The property is up for sale and has been empty for about three months. She then shouted for her husband, who'd been sitting watching the television in the front room. When he came through, he saw the light too. He slipped on his jacket and shoes and went over to have a look. Next thing she remembers is that she heard him calling her name, and when she went out, he was staggering back along the garden path with blood streaming down his face. Said he'd seen a man in there, but he had a balaclava on. When the man saw him looking in through the kitchen window, he came out and attacked him with something solid, doesn't know what, but he just ran. The wife then rang 999.'

Burton nodded. 'So, Simon, you then went to take a look?' He looked towards Banks, who had now laid his head back down on the pillow and looked like he was about to close his eyes at any second. That being the case he thought that he'd better ask his next question quickly. 'And what did you see?'

'Not much, sir,' Banks sprung to life again and raised his head again on hearing his name. 'Jane took a look around the front and I went around the back. The next thing I knew, something hard hit me on the head and I felt something stuck into my side. I called for Jane and that's all I can remember. I think I must have passed out.'

'And I rang 999 and kept pressing onto his side wound until the ambulance arrived,' she said. 'One of Mrs Markham's daughters arrived just as we were leaving for the hospital. I think she was taking Mrs Markham in to see her husband.'

'Okay, thanks you two. You both did a good job last night,' Burton said. Rising from the chair, he put a hand on Banks's shoulder. 'I had planned to go and have a word with Mr Markham, but after what you've said about the burglar wearing a mask, I doubt if he can tell me any more than you have. Take it easy, Simon, and get plenty of rest. You're okay and that's all that matters right now.'

'Thanks, boss.' He tried hard to suppress a yawn but failed.

Burton saw that as his cue to take his leave and give Jane Francis a lift home before he headed off home himself to relieve his refrigerator of one of the bottles of beer.

14

After leaving the station, Fielding went home to quickly pack for the journey back up to her native north east. As per usual, as soon as she entered her hallway, she was greeted by her two cats, Sooty and Sweep, who did their customary circling around and through her legs in figure of eight movements, purring loudly as they performed their nightly dance. She'd rescued the two siblings three years ago following their owner's death on one of her cases. She had instantly fallen in love with them and decided to keep them rather than hand them in to the RSPCA. This is what should have happened when animals were found left in a house, but she just couldn't do it. Both were Maine Coon crosses: Sooty had white fur with 'sooty' smudges all over her, whereas Sweep was all grey in colour. They had both been an important part of her way of life ever since their adoption.

'Hello, you two!' she said to them, taking turns to stroke them both. 'Come on then, I'll feed you.' They followed her into the kitchen where she replenished both their food and water bowls. They seemed to instinctively sense that she was not staying for long as they stared questioningly at her while she prepared their morning food in the timer feeders. She likewise put one of the living room lights on a timer switch. Cats are sensitive creatures and they knew that something was up. She caught them staring at her in the way only cats can do.

'Yes, I'm going out again,' she told them, bending down and giving them an extra stroke apiece, 'but I'll be back tomorrow, don't you worry!' She felt sure that they understood every word that she said and were chastising her. 'Oh, don't look at me like that!' She laughed.

Before calling for a taxi, she dug her small suitcase out from underneath the bed and gathered together everything she needed for an overnight stay, primarily a fresh change of clothing and toiletries. She felt certain that the hotel would provide hair dryers and bathrobes, if she found that she needed to use them, so there was no need to overcrowd her case with unnecessary things like that. When the cab arrived, she bid farewell to her precious feline twosome, promising to see them soon, and left for the airport. She knew that Claire would be doing likewise; they had arranged to meet in the airport lounge at seven for the 7.30 flight up to Newcastle upon Tyne International Airport. In the cab, she took a moment to check the arrangements for their flight and hotel accommodation that a member of the administrative staff had made before she left work.

The flight up to Newcastle was a relatively short one, and Fielding and Claire managed to reconnect to one another during that time.

When they'd settled into their seats, one of the first things Claire had said to her was, 'I see that you're still not using your first name then!'

Fielding laughed. 'You know, I've used my middle name for so long now, it's just second nature to me. Don't get me wrong though, I love my given name, always have done. I think I decided to go with my middle one just to rebel against my mother.' It wasn't quite the truth, but she'd told herself that this was the reason for so long, she'd come to believe it.

'Yes, I was so sorry about your father. I remember you went through a really bad time back then. Still not on speaking terms with your mother or sister then?'

'No,' Fielding confessed. 'Neither of them can forgive me for wanting to follow in Dad's footsteps. I, in turn, cannot forgive them for being so unsupportive in my choice of career. If it was good enough for Dad then it's certainly good enough for me.'

Claire took a drink from her bottle of water. 'Well maybe they'll change their mind one day.'

Fielding shook her head. 'No, I doubt that.' Both her mother and her sister had made that abundantly clear to her before she'd left for Manchester.

* * *

They'd been booked into two single rooms at the Britannia Hotel, which was just a short walk from the airport. Despite memories from the past, Fielding had to admit that it felt good to be back in her own neck of the woods again. She'd missed it over the years, but had now become part of the whole Manchester scene, and had spent a lot of time over the past thirteen years with her dad's relatives who lived in and around the area. Just another thing to alienate her from her mother and sister, it seemed, as they'd never seen a great deal of dad's side of the family before his untimely death. On top of everything else, Fielding knew her mother and sister had seen her move to Manchester as taking sides against them. They'd have preferred her to stay in the north east, pursuing a career more suited to them, rather than the one she had chosen for herself.

Her main reason for deciding to study in Manchester had been a purely personal one, as she could have easily become a police officer in the north east, putting up with her mother's and sister's opposition. But no, her boyfriend at the time, Bobby Samson, had been accepted at the University of Manchester to study economics and politics and she'd gone down there to be with him, studying not far away at Sedgley Park Police Academy. They'd even moved into accommodation together, sharing a flat between their two places of study until, after only the space of a few months, Bobby's eye had been turned by another student on his course. Fielding had found them together one evening in their home and in their bed. She'd gathered together her things right there and then and left them to it, finding somewhere else to live for the duration of her studies.

She'd dated on and off after that, but nothing serious as her trust in men had been seriously and irrevocably damaged that night. It wasn't until she'd joined Burton's team that she began to have faith in men again. He had restored that for her through his words and his actions. They'd never been anything other than colleagues, but she felt that there was this unspoken thing between them that would remain unspoken for as long as they were colleagues – which was probably going to be a long time to come.

Their appointment at police headquarters was for 9.30 the next morning. Fielding was ready and waiting when Claire knocked on her door at 7.45, and together they had breakfast in the restaurant downstairs before getting reception to call them a taxi for their meeting with the police commissioner, William Trenton, in the Cobalt Business Centre offices in North Tyneside.

Trenton was a distinguished-looking man with silvery-grey hair and a neatly trimmed moustache. He looked years younger than the sixty-two years she knew him to be. He thanked them for coming on such short notice, then quickly moved on to the business in hand. Pressing the intercom on his desk, he spoke to his secretary and asked her to send in a DCI Winters with all the relevant information for them.

'We could have sent all this down to you,' DCI Winters said to Fielding and Rawlins when they were both standing with him at the table in front of the window, 'but we've been having issues with our external courier services so have had to stop sending documents this way for the time being.' The two sets of files he had brought in with him, both the Northumbria Police ones and the Manchester ones, had been opened and reports and photographs were now spread across the entire length of the table. Claire Rawlins was busy reading the medical examiner's report, but it was the two crime scene photographs from up here that caught Fielding's attention.

'We drew a complete blank when we were trying to solve this case and had no leads whatsoever to go on apart from these.' Winters pointed to what had already caught Fielding's attention. 'We had to leave the case open for the sake of the victims' families, but really thought that this was going to be one of the unsolved ones. Then we got wind of what had been happening down in your neck of the woods in Manchester, and it was the break we were looking for.'

Fielding picked up the two photographs and showed them to Rawlins, who was still engrossed in the medical reports. Both women exchanged glances: two playing cards, both the queen of hearts, and a partial thumb print in the bottom left-hand corner captured for all time and preserved with the black forensic dust.

'They're the same as the ones we have,' Fielding told Winters, 'but the cards we have with our victims are the joker, the ace of spades and the queen of clubs.'

'As you can imagine,' Winters continued, 'we couldn't believe our luck when the two separate cases cross-referenced themselves. Although the term "luck" seems a bit tasteless, considering.'

'I can't see why your two victims had the same playing card beside them, though,' Fielding stated, looking at all the sets of photographs laid out in front of her now. 'At first we thought that the cards were linked to the way each of the victims were found. Mr Jackson in fancy dress – like a joker maybe? Mr Stephenson in his allotment – we could see a definite link to the spade card. Then Ms Johnson's head was completely decimated by a club – hence the queen of clubs. But these two,' Fielding motioned to the two north east victims, 'were they missing their hearts?'

'Not at all, although we had noticed that possible connection too,' Winters told her. 'What we had were a decapitation and a drowning, but the drowning victim had been sedated first; we found a similar needle injection site at the base of the neck – just like your victims.'

'But not the decapitated victim?' Fielding asked.

'No. We think that there was no need to sedate her as the beheading would have been instant. Therefore... no need.'

A chill went through Fielding as she contemplated the scene. This was no ordinary killer; he, or she even, as that was indeed a possibility, had no qualms whatsoever to either mutilate to the point of non-recognition, or behead another human being. It was cold and very calculated; extremely so, especially as a calling card had been left beside each of the victims' bodies. But the definitive link between them was now wide open again. Northumbria Police's victims were not in education, and they were both in their late twenties, exactly the same age as one another and, as Fielding observed, her own age too.

It was then that Rawlins spoke up after a long spell of silence, and completely changed the direction of the inquiry. 'I know these two people.' She was looking at the pre-death photographs of Jennifer Grayson and Caroline Porter. Then she turned to Fielding and added, 'And so do you, Fielding.'

15

'W hat?' Fielding looked very closely at the photographs of the two women. She hadn't been back to her native north east for around thirteen years. How could she possibly know them? Rawlins lived and worked up here, so it was more likely for her to know them than Fielding herself.

'Maybe you find them familiar but I don't think I do.' Fielding scrutinised their features closely but nothing remotely familiar jumped back at her.

'Yes you do,' Rawlins insisted. 'They were both at school with us. You were close friends with them as I remember. Only then, Jennifer Grayson was Jennifer Sanderson.'

Fielding looked again. Younger versions of both women formed in her mind. Jennifer Sanderson, with long dark hair way past her waistline, and the longest lashes she had ever seen on anyone – even on models in magazines. Then there was Caroline Porter, who was slightly overweight, but with bright green eyes the colour of jade and short auburn hair cut in a fashionable pixie-style. Could they be the same two as the faces she was looking at now? The faces of her one-time close friends?

'If that's the case, then this is very significant,' Commissioner Trenton finally spoke as he joined them at the table. 'You say that you have a possible suspect down in Manchester?'

'He works up here during the week, but it's beginning to look as if he may be our main suspect now,' Fielding told him. Adding, 'Were both these women murdered on a weekday by any chance?'

Claire Fielding still had the medical reports on both the victims and checked for the recorded dates of death. 'Yes,' she said after carefully checking both of them. 'They died on a Wednesday and a Thursday.'

'Then I would say that you have quite a substantial case against this nephew,' the Commissioner concluded.

Fielding rang Burton to break the news to him. As it was a Saturday, Carruthers should be back at his home in Manchester and she felt that this may just well be enough to bring him in for questioning. She had already asked for the information in the files to be emailed down to Manchester, and Claire Rawlins had asked for the forensic information to be sent directly to Dr Barnes at the coroner's office. She also rang him to tell him that the information would be arriving by fax shortly, doubtless ruining his Saturday morning lie-in.

'Oh, and Fielding,' Burton had added before ending the conversation, 'can you go out to the place where Carruthers works up there? I know that Northumbria Police have visited him already, but that was to check he was there this week. Can you go and see the manager personally, and get him to also check his records for the dates the two women were killed up there. I believe that the place is open at the weekends. Ask him what Carruthers is like while you're there. Is he liked, is he not liked, is he trustworthy, you know the sort of thing.'

Also taking copies of the files for them to scrutinise on the flight home, Fielding and Rawlins thanked DCI Winters and the police commissioner for all the information they had provided them with

and waited for the call back from Burton from the comfort of Star-
bucks café at The Village Hotel on the Cobalt Business Park site. At
11am, Burton called Fielding to confirm that Carruthers was now
sitting quite unhappily in the comfort of one of their cells and
awaiting his solicitor. He had confirmed his place of employment to
be a company called ComputerLinks, which operated out of the
Tyne Tunnel Trading Estate just a mile or so away from the Cobalt,
and was open on a Saturday... and the manager was now expecting
them.

'We should have hired a car,' Rawlins said as they sat in the taxi.
'Or I could have gone home and got mine.'

'Where are you living now then?' Fielding asked, thinking that it
might have been a good idea if she'd mentioned it earlier.

'I'm in Whitley Bay, not far from the seafront.'

Fielding remembered her trips to North Tyneside when she was
younger. Whitley Bay was quite the place to go back then, made
even more popular by the fact that one of the members of the pop
group Duran Duran was from there and had a wine bar in the town.
But perhaps the big drawing point to the area, apart from the lure of
a local pop star's bar and the hope of a glimpse of him there, was the
Spanish City – an outside fun fair and games arcade, originally
erected way back in the early twentieth century to be a smaller
version of the iconic Blackpool Pleasure Beach. Together with the
Blackpool-like array of fish and chip shops and slot machines on
every corner, it was the go-to place during the summer months. She
had loved it there in the summer with her friends. The same two
friends who were now part of a police investigation into their
murders.

'It's been restored recently,' Rawlins said as Fielding reminisced
about her childhood spent in Whitley Bay. 'Quite the place to go
these days, completely renovated and housing restaurants and
leisure facilities. They've even got a champagne bar in there too.'

She appreciated the march of progress in her native part of the country, but all her wonderful memories of the place disappeared in an instant. It had all gone, never to be seen again. A bit like her one-time friends.

It didn't take too long for them to get to the ComputerLinks site, and to save time afterwards, they asked the taxi driver if he would wait for them.

The manager, a Mr Barry Sangster, was extremely concerned to hear that they were asking him about Alex Carruthers. 'Alex? What's he done then?' he asked while checking the attendance logs for the dates he'd been given.

'We're just hoping that he can help us with our enquiries, sir,' Fielding told him, not willing to say that he now appeared to be the prime suspect in their murder case.

'Enquiries?' He stopped looking at the computer screen and faced them.

'Didn't he tell you about what happened in Manchester?' she asked.

He shook his head, looking even more concerned now than he had been before.

'His great-uncle was murdered.'

A look of genuine shock appeared on the manager's face.

Now why wouldn't Carruthers have mentioned something like that? Unless he was, as Burton had said after he'd spoken to him, something of an 'insensitive arse'. Burton hadn't liked him, and if Burton didn't like someone, it usually meant that there was something questionable about them or their behaviour. And Fielding trusted his judgement implicitly.

'I... I didn't know...' he spluttered. 'He just didn't mention it.'

'Does he seem a secretive sort of person to you at all?' Fielding continued.

Sangster didn't need to think about that one. 'No, not at all. A little overly-sharing if you ask me; won't shut up half the time. It's not like him to keep quiet about something like that... and it's his own flesh and blood as well, isn't it? I'm very surprised. You'd think he'd want to talk about it, or have time off even...' he trailed off.

'What sort of person is he then?' Rawlins decided to join in with the questioning. Fielding cast her a sideways glance. Usually she wouldn't tolerate a civilian butting into her enquiries, but as Rawlins was there on official police business, albeit in a civilian capacity, she let it pass... this time.

'Well, he's a good enough bloke, I suppose.' Sangster almost seemed reluctant to say it.

'I sense a "but" there,' Fielding said, noticing his hesitation.

'Can't fault him with the work; he certainly knows what he's doing with computers. So he should, all the qualifications he has. He was sent up from head office down in Manchester to help us open the branch here. But as for him personally...' He trailed off momentarily. 'Well, how can I say this politely?'

'Just say it, sir,' Fielding encouraged.

'He's such a dick. Arrogant little prick. The girls seem to like him, but he's not a man's man, if you know what I mean. No offence, but he's not a "northern" bloke – not one of the boys.' He then remembered that he was talking to a police officer from Manchester – hardly local, hardly 'northern' as he had put it. But then he was confused, for he did notice a local accent from both of them. He decided to stop there and not say any more – probably best. Eyes now back on the computer screen, it didn't take long for him to find the information Fielding had asked for.

'Right, here we are,' he said, pointing to the screen, and Fielding leaned in to take a look. 'Yes, he was here on both those dates.'

There was one last question Fielding felt obliged to ask him. 'And when he's working up here, does he ever leave the office, go out for an hour or two – anything like that?'

Sangster laughed. 'Like I said, he's a dick; goes off whenever he feels like it. Thinks he's God's gift to mankind, the jumped up little...'

But Fielding cut him short. 'Okay, thank you, sir.' She got the picture.

16

Even though things weren't looking that good for Carruthers, Fielding had to admit to herself – and Burton the next time that she spoke to him – that he couldn't have killed anybody in Manchester this week as he was working in the north east at ComputerLinks, just confirmed by Barry Sangster, the manager.

In any case, what could the possible motive be for him to kill two women, both known to Fielding herself in her youth. It just didn't make any sense at all. This was turning out to be one of the most baffling cases both she and Burton had ever experienced in their careers on the force. It really wasn't the best time for Rawlins to ask her if she wanted to visit her mother.

'Why on earth would I want to do that?' Fielding asked with perhaps more venom than she had intended to.

'Whoa, steady!' Rawlins put her hands up in defence. 'I just thought that, as you are up here, you might want to go and see her, that's all.'

'I haven't wanted to see either her or my sister since I left here over thirteen years ago. What could possibly possess me to want to do so now?'

'Okay, sorry I brought it up.' Rawlins's apology seemed genuine enough, and Fielding now felt guilty for exploding that way in front of her. This case was definitely getting to her and her outburst had been unforgivable.

'No, I'm the one who's sorry, Claire,' she apologised. 'Ah, it's this case. I don't know if you know this but we'd just closed one case before this one came along, and I thought that was a really tough one. We could have done with a week or two's break before getting into something like that again.'

'Could another team of detectives not take over the reins for you?'

'No, not at all. Heaven forbid. It's Burton's baby, and once he gets his teeth into something, nobody can take it from him. I know he's just as beat as I am, probably more so, but he doesn't give up... at all... ever.'

'Well I hope you find a resolution for this one pretty soon. I can tell that you – in fact all of your team, not just you and Burton – are on edge with it.'

* * *

'I'm sorry to have to ask you to do this, Fielding,' Burton said on the telephone when he rang her shortly afterwards, 'but can I ask you, while you're up there, to go along to Franklin Electronics in Boldon Business Park and speak to the owner there about Jennifer Grayson. I've already spoken to him and he's expecting you. And can you also have a word with the late Caroline Porter's neighbour in Cleadon? Her name's Sandra Matthews – and she's a "Miss" apparently, made a point of saying that at the time she was interviewed. Ask about Carruthers, show them both a picture. Also show them the sketch artist's drawing. See if either have been seen around the area over the past few months. In fact, ask them if they've seen anybody or anything suspicious during that time. I know it's a couple of months back now, and memories can fade, but let's give it a shot. I've only got a short window to hold Carruthers here, and his solicitor is a right piece of work.'

'So's Carruthers by the sound of it.' Fielding told Burton all about what Barry Sangster had said about his company's computer wizard.

Burton had responded with, 'Sounds about right.'

Ending the call, Fielding turned to Claire Rawlins and said, 'You know your offer of the car?'

Rawlins nodded, saying, 'It's still on if you want it.'

'Yes,' Fielding told her. 'I think it might be a good idea; we're not finished quite yet up here.'

*　*　*

Burton had only just finished the call to Fielding when there was a knock on his door. He shouted, 'Come in,' and Wayman's head appeared from around the door, then the rest of him.

'Can I have a word, sir?' he asked, and Burton indicated for him to sit.

'What is it, Sam?'

'Well, sir, it's that house in Altrincham, the one where Simon was injured...' Wayman seemed troubled by the information he was about to impart.

'What about it?'

'You're not going to believe this!'

Although holding it back, Burton was growing mildly impatient. This was turning into a guessing game and he really wasn't in the mood right now to be playing games of any sort. However, when he said, 'Just spit it out,' it did come out a little more harshly than intended and he regretted it as soon as it was said.

Wayman, feeling as if he'd just said something wrong, sat himself up a little straighter in the chair.

'Sorry, Sam, this thing is getting to all of us,' Burton apologised, hoping that his DC would get to the point quickly as there was so much more he needed to be doing.

'Well,' Wayman hurried it along now, 'it's just that the house is up on the market because its owner went to live in a care home three months ago.'

Burton edged forward in his seat, sensing exactly where this was about to go next, 'Don't tell me...' he began, but Wayman finished his sentence for him.

'Yes, it's Nathaniel Jackson's old house.'

'That's not just a coincidence then, is it?' Phillipa Preston astutely observed when Burton followed Wayman back into the incident room and gathered them around to relate this interesting piece of information.

'No, I wouldn't have thought so.'

'Well, it couldn't have been Carruthers as he was working up in the north east,' Francis informed everyone.

'There's only one other thing possible then,' Burton announced to all the group. He didn't need the help of a profiler to work this one out. 'If Carruthers is involved in this, then there must be someone else working with him.'

As if realising that DI Burton was doing her job for her, Louise Simmons spoke up, voicing something which had been on her mind since hearing about the murders up north. 'The murders up in Newcastle have made me think of another option, of course.' She looked around at all the group.

'Which is?' Burton would be more than happy to hear any suggestions or options right now.

'If we consider all the murders to be linked in some way, which seems more than reasonable to assume now when we take the cards into account – we now have a total of five, both here in Manchester and up in the Newcastle area, and if we take Carruthers out of the picture there is one other person to connect them all.'

'Yes, there's our John Doe,' Burton stated.

But Simmons continued with, 'No, not him.'

Burton couldn't for the life of him see what she was getting at, nor could the rest of his team, judging by the blank looks on all their faces. The only other person who could possibly be involved in this was the unknown person who had been visiting the care home.

Seeing that she needed to elaborate on her statement, Simmons simply said, 'Sally Fielding.'

'Fielding!' Burton exclaimed. 'How on earth have you come to that conclusion?'

'It's the two murders in the north east that made me think about it. Another card is left at the scene of the killings, the queen of hearts on both occasions, and both women were known to Fielding, and from her old home town. From the way I see it,' Simmons continued, explaining how she'd come to this conclusion, 'perhaps it's to do with a case she worked on in the past and someone is getting back at her by killing her friends?'

'That's logical enough, I presume.' Burton could hear what she was saying, but was finding the whole idea too extraordinary to comprehend, 'but I think that suggestion has just made the reasons behind the killings even more complicated than before.'

Phillipa Preston offered up her opinion. 'I can see what you mean, Louise, especially about the playing cards, and I can get what the connection might be to Fielding with regard to the north east murders, but, like the DI has suggested, how can this possibly be linked to the murders here in Manchester? They can't possibly be... yet they seem to be.' She paused momentarily trying to take all of this in. 'This whole thing just seems to sit right somehow.'

'I know what you mean,' agreed Burton, trying to get his head around this new revelation as well.

'Right,' he said after a couple of minutes of reflection. 'Gather together all the information we have and we'll get the DCI down here to take a look at this. Maybe we need a fresh set of eyes on this… although, this one's beyond me. In the meantime, Summers, you're with me. I think we need to pay a visit to Nathaniel Jackson's house in Altrincham.'

* * *

Claire Rawlins's house in Whitley Bay was more new build than old traditional and, as she had said, quite close to the seafront. So close, in fact, that when they both alighted from the taxi on the main road by the gates, Fielding could smell the ozone in the air. She always felt that she'd grown up along the north east coastline, but her village was just under three miles from the North Sea. Here, Claire was just a very short distance from the long golden sands and the crashing waves. Even though the winter was fast approaching and the colder dark nights had already begun to set in, the air was crisp and vigorously refreshing.

'Great, isn't it?' Claire said, seeing the look on Fielding's face as she took in her surroundings. 'It's not just the sea air that's making your cheeks glow so much!'

'Oh, this is so lovely, Claire,' Fielding declared, looking around her. She'd almost forgotten how harsh and yet so beautiful her homeland was, having lived in Manchester for so many years.

'See what you've been missing!' Rawlins laughed, leading the way up the driveway.

The inside of the house was not disappointing either. Very fresh and modern with a distinct Scandinavian feel to it, it was minimal but not excessively so. Lovely little touches littered the place, like colourful cushions and unusual prints on the walls. Fielding thought it was how she would like her place in Manchester to look, but she had to admit that she seemed to have accumulated a lot more odds and ends than Claire had – unless, of course, she had a spare room somewhere that she could just push everything in until she wanted them. Fielding didn't have the luxury of a spare room, or a loft, so all that she owned shared the space with herself and her two cats. A bit cramped perhaps, but she'd made it as cosy as she could and it was the place she looked forward to coming home to and settling down in every night.

While Claire went off in search of her car keys, Fielding looked at the array of photographs on the shelving. The frame of the shelving unit was a large A shape, with four shelves within the main structure, and it was something that she would have liked for her own place as a quirky reference to her own first name. There were four framed photographs of Claire with her parents, one of her in her graduation cap and gown, proudly holding up a degree certificate, and the last one was a photo of her with a man who was about the same age as she was.

Claire re-entered the room dangling a set of car keys from her finger. Fielding thought that an odd look crossed her old friend's face when she saw her looking at the last photograph but it quickly passed and she said, 'You ready then?'

'Who's the man?' Fielding asked her, picking the photograph up to look at it more closely.

'It's... he's just a friend of mine.' She came across to take it from Fielding's hands and replaced it where it had sat before.

Fielding got the message instantly and let it go. Claire obviously didn't want to talk to her about him so she left it at that. Was he a boyfriend? Had he been a boyfriend and they'd parted? Whoever he was, it seemed from his place on her shelving that it was somebody that she cared about very much. Only thing was, Claire just didn't seem to want to discuss him with her.

Things had changed a great deal in the past thirteen years, although the Boldon and Cleadon areas appeared to be very much the same as she'd remembered them, Fielding thought as she sat in the passenger seat next to Rawlins. The Business Park, however, was doing more business than she remembered, and looked to be the hub of the local community, with the cinema complex, the surrounding restaurants and fast food outlets doing a roaring trade judging by the number of people and families now gathering in and around them.

Franklin Electronics was near the back of Boldon Business Park, quite a distance away from the road. It was an impressive glass-fronted building which gave way to a bigger enclosed warehouse behind that. The company's European manager, John Scott, was sitting in his office just right of the main front door. He rose to his feet when he saw them pull into the car park.

As if on cue, the minute Rawlins turned off the car's ignition, Fielding's phone pinged to let her know that a message had come through. *Bad timing, Joe,* she thought. He had texted:

`Give me a call when you can.`

But as he hadn't said that it was urgent, it would have to wait now until she and Rawlins had spoken to Mr Scott.

'How well did you know Jennifer Grayson, Mr Scott?' Fielding asked him when they were seated in his office. As offices go, it was a very nice one: spacious, with an abundance of natural light, and a large table at the opposite end to his desk, big enough to sit maybe twenty people. A television almost as large as the table sat high on the wall behind it.

'She'd been working at the company for almost seven years. Worked her way up from an office temp to being my deputy. She was a lovely person, and so is her husband. I just can't imagine what he's going through right now, especially with the little boy.'

Fielding felt a chill run right through her. She'd been very close to Jennifer at school, and felt guilty at that moment that she hadn't kept in touch. But with moving away, and then getting the job in Manchester, her old life up here just seemed to take second place. The row she'd had with her mother and sister hadn't helped matters... but she really should have kept in touch with her friends from her school days.

She continued her questioning, trying to put regret to the back of her mind. 'Had there been anyone hanging around the place, acting suspiciously, or did you know if anyone had been pestering Jennifer for any reason?'

'No... no... that's just the thing. Jennifer got on well with everybody she knew. As far as I am aware she had no enemies. Nobody that would do... that... to her. She was one of the nicest people I've ever met, she really was.'

At that point, Fielding brought the two photographs out of the file she had on her lap. 'I wonder if you recognise any of these people, sir?' She laid the photos of Alex Carruthers and John Doe out in front of him.

He carefully scrutinised both images before pointing at Carruthers. Fielding's pulse began to race. Could this be the break that they were after?

'I think I recognise him from the newspapers the other night... does he have something to do with this?'

'Have you ever seen him here or lurking around, or did Jennifer know him perhaps?'

'No,' still looking at the face in front of him. 'I've never seen him before, only in the papers like I said. I know most, if not all of Jennifer's friends, and I can honestly say that he's not one of them.'

Severely let down but not wishing to show it, Fielding simply told him that they needed him to get in touch with them about another matter and left it at that.

'I thought we were really onto something there,' Rawlins said to Fielding as she was fastening her seat belt back in the car. 'He seemed pretty definite though, didn't he?'

'Yes,' she replied, locking herself in as well. 'We'll try Caroline Porter's neighbour in Cleadon. She's our last hope up here, and if she gives us the same answer as John Scott, then I doubt if we can pin anything on Alex Carruthers for these two murders.'

Claire was driving now. 'I think he's a good bet for his great-uncle though, don't you think? Everything seems to point to him.'

Fielding had to admit that he was – in fact, he was the only suspect they had, full stop. And as for John Doe... well... whoever he was and whatever he had to do with this, nobody seemed to know anything about him, and he hadn't come forward either.

As they drove through the impressive Tyne Tunnel, the underwater carriageway beneath the River Tyne linking the counties of North and South Tyneside, and out towards Cleadon, Sally Fielding's childhood memories of the place came flooding back to her. Lovely memories prior to the death of her father; not so happy afterwards.

17

A gaudy red and black estate agent's sign sticking out at an angle from the unkempt hedge read Whitlock and Sons, and included a telephone number in a sickly yellow colour on the bottom line. Burton rang the number and waited. Saturday morning, somebody should be there, and on the sixth ring the call was picked up by a youngish-sounding girl. He quickly introduced himself and explained the basics of the situation. She then put him momentarily on hold while she went to get her manager who was, as she put it, 'in the back office'.

'How may I help you, detective?' This was the voice of an older woman this time and, unfortunately, he had to go through everything again with her. He was a bit annoyed at the young girl for not passing the message on. Listening to what he said, the manager, whose name was Miss Jameson, said that she would immediately drive out to meet them with the key to the property. She was true to her word and arrived well within fifteen minutes of the call.

'So who else has a key to the place?' Burton had asked the estate agent before entering. 'Is it his great-nephew, Alex Carruthers?'

'He does have one, I believe,' Miss Jameson confirmed, 'although we haven't seen him since Mr Jackson left the property.'

'What about any other relatives? Did Mr Jackson have anyone else apart from him?'

'Yes, I believe he did,' the woman recalled. 'I'll have to look it up when I get back to the office, but there are other relatives as far as I can remember.'

Asking if she wouldn't mind waiting outside, at least until they'd taken a look around, Burton and Summers donned their nitrile gloves and entered the property. The bungalow was cold when they entered, perhaps to be expected for a building which had stood empty for the past three months, and made even more so by the wintery chill that was in the air today.

It was decorated in a style Burton would have attributed to an older person with more traditional tastes. It reminded him of the way his grandmother would have had it, all floral wallpaper and high wing-back chairs, and an old-fashioned gas fire in the living room sitting on a tiled hearth. Bungalows were popular and always snapped up quickly, but not this one apparently, and that was most likely down to the decor and furnishings. Weren't you supposed to empty a house completely when you were trying to sell it these days, or were you supposed to redecorate it to make it more appealing?

Burton noticed a broken glass pane in the rear door, which he would bring to the attention of the estate agent, but other than that nothing seemed to be out of place until Summers called him into the living room.

'In here, sir!'

'Yes, what is it?' Burton asked, following the sound of Summers's voice.

'There's a photograph missing from this frame here,' Summers stated, pointing to the one which was lying face up at the end of a row. Burton went across and looked at all the photographs arranged on the sideboard. Anyone giving them a quick glance would have easily missed it.

'Well done, Jack,' he said to his DC, then proceeded to examine each in turn. There were a few of Mr Jackson with a woman who must have been his wife, and a couple of him with a group of men, and also an old black and white photograph of him in an RAF uniform. He went outside and asked the estate agent to come in and take a look. 'I don't suppose you can remember what was in this frame here?' he asked holding the now empty frame up for her to see.

She shook her head, 'No, I'm sorry, I really don't. You'll have to speak to Mr Carruthers about that.'

Oh I will, thought Burton, bringing a poly bag out of his pocket and slipping the frame into it.

* * *

Sally Fielding remembered most, if not all of the houses in Cleadon Village being larger than average. Even the bungalows were mostly dormer ones which had been redesigned with loft conversions and extensions. The village was also home to a lot of people who either owned horses or were horse-riding enthusiasts. That was one thing that she remembered very clearly about the place, the horse riders parading throughout the village and surrounding areas either on the roads or along the bridle paths. Even a paddock full of horses every size and colour marked the imaginary boundary line division between the semi-rural villages of East Boldon and Cleadon. Miss Sandra Matthews lived in one of the above average-sized bungalows just off the main road which stretched from one end of Cleadon to the other.

'I don't really know what I can tell you that I haven't already told the police,' Miss Matthews said, leading them into her beloved conservatory and indicating that they take a seat on the double rattan sofa. Her dog, Sammy, had been running rings around himself in the garden outside prior to their arrival but stopped when he saw two strangers with his owner and started to run back towards the conservatory, barking frantically. He stopped just in front of the door and stopped barking when he saw that she was not in any sort of danger.

'Lovely dog,' Rawlins said. 'He seems very loyal.'

'Oh he is,' Miss Matthews confirmed. 'In fact, it was Sammy who alerted me to what happened to the poor girl next door in the first place.'

'Yes, we read your statement,' Fielding told her, 'but you yourself didn't hear anything at all that day?'

'No, I didn't, I'm sorry to say. I did think that she had just slipped and fallen at first, but she was very cold by the time I got there. I used to be a nurse, and I could tell that she had been dead for quite some time. Somebody must have put her out there. Though, Sammy wouldn't have barked as much as he did if he hadn't heard somebody – you saw him when he saw you two come in here.'

'And what about these two men – have you seen either of them before? Maybe coming to see Miss Porter or perhaps in or around the village?' Fielding showed her the two photographs of Carruthers and John Doe.

Miss Matthews studied them intently, but finally said that she hadn't seen them or anyone who looked like them. 'Caroline didn't have many visitors, come to think of it. She seemed to go out to see friends rather than have them come around to hers. Nice girl, it was such a shame. I can't think why anyone would want to harm her.'

'One final question, if you don't mind?' Fielding said, drawing the meeting to a close. 'Can you tell me what your neighbour did for a living?'

'Yes, of course. She worked for an insurance company in the middle of Sunderland city centre. Must have been there for quite a while as it's the only job I've known her to have had since she's been here.'

'So there's no link to education that you know of?' Fielding felt that she was clutching at straws, but thought that she'd better ask the lady while she was there.

'Oh, now, funny you should say that, detective.'

Fielding's interest sparked and she cast a glance in Rawlins's direction, to which Rawlins raised her eyebrows. 'Oh,' Fielding replied, 'why is that?'

Miss Matthews continued, 'She was a school governor.'

'But I thought that she wasn't married?' Rawlins asked, assuming like most that, in order to achieve that elevated position in education, it was necessary to have a child in the school you were a governor of.

'No, she wasn't,' Miss Matthews confirmed, 'but she was one of the governors in the school in West Boldon where her cousin's son is a pupil.'

Almost afraid to ask, Fielding continued to probe, 'And what is her cousin's name, Miss Matthews?'

'Why it's Peter, Peter Grayson.'

'Is that the Peter Grayson whose wife was murdered in Boldon Business Park at around the same time?' Rawlins asked her.

'Why... yes it is, come to think of it.' Then an expression of realisation crossed Miss Matthews' face. 'Oh my goodness, you don't think the two deaths were related... do you? That's terrible. I didn't make the connection at the time, but... oh my goodness...'

Fielding really didn't want to reveal too much at all to her but felt obliged to say something, especially as she had now just given the woman quite a shock, it seemed. 'We don't quite know at the moment, but it may be a possibility.'

As both Fielding and Rawlins left Miss Matthews in perhaps a worse state than when they first saw her, they then felt obliged to follow up one final thing, bearing in mind the latest revelation on the case. Fielding retrieved John Scott's business card from her warrant card holder and dialled his number. His answer, although not the one she really wanted to hear, was perhaps now not unexpected.

'Yes, she was,' was his simple reply to the question of whether or not Jennifer Grayson was a school governor.

Fielding dialled another number, this time to Joe Burton to tell him the latest news.

18

'I want each and every one of you to go home after this,' Detective Chief Inspector Ambleton said to everyone in the room, 'and not come back in until Monday morning.'

'I don't think that's possible...' Burton began but was stopped in his tracks by the DCI.

'When I say everyone should go home, I mean everyone... and that includes yourself, detective inspector.'

Burton felt like a child being chastised in front of his teacher. His team had prepared a big presentation for her, had gathered together all the facts they had on the case, which had now grown to a massive five murders if he took the ones in the north east into account. They had hoped that by coming together for this meeting, they might just end up with something productive. He couldn't see the point in arguing with her, so just said to everyone, 'Okay, let's get this up and running. And don't forget, if you have any ideas or suggestions, or see something that nobody has thought of before, just speak up and let us hear it. We need to get on top of this today.'

DCI Ambleton had known Joe Burton for a long time, and knew exactly what he was capable of. If he wasn't such a good detective, then he would have already passed the authority on to Fielding and taken a day's leave, but she knew that he wasn't that sort of person. He was like a hungry dog with a bone. Once he got his teeth into something, he would never let go of it until he was through. She also knew that he needed a break just as much as his team did, and although she wasn't showing it herself, she was as much perplexed by this case as he was. He most definitely needed a day off to gather all his wits together, as she could see that he was flagging with this more and more as each day passed, and there was nothing more ineffective than a burnt-out detective.

'Right.' Burton had them all sitting around the table in one of the conference rooms. He missed Fielding, but had Phillipa Preston stand in for her on this occasion. Although Ambleton had instructed the entire team to go home that evening and not return until Monday, he'd doubtless be in touch with Fielding either later that night when she got home or the next day to bring her up to speed. 'Let's see what we have so far,' he continued and walked across to the projector screen on the wall across from where they were all sitting, and he nodded towards Preston to start up the presentation on her computer.

The first image appeared on the screen. From left to right: a photograph of Nathaniel Jackson, dressed in his 'clown' outfit, as Fielding had put it; to its right, Jacob Stephenson sitting in his picnic chair outside his shed at the allotment, head right back and his mouth crammed full of sweets; and finally the body of Dorothy Johnson with the photograph only showing the prone body from the back of the neck down – fortunately the head, or lack of it, had been excluded from the shot, which was a blessing for all concerned. Underneath each of the photographs was the matching playing card, each still in its poly bag, which had been found at the scene of each crime.

Everyone stared at the images again. They had looked at them so many times over the past few days, but Burton was hoping that maybe, just maybe, the DCI might pick up on something which they had missed.

Directing his attention to Ambleton, Burton began to go through the case piece by piece. 'We have three people killed in very different ways, but with three definite links – all three were in education prior to their retirement, all three were apparently subdued prior to their death as a syringe mark was found at the base of the neck, and a playing card was left at the scene of each crime. Mr Jackson's strange apparel was not his clothing, nor was it the clothing of any of the residents in the care home. Therefore it was brought in and put on him for a specific reason by the person who killed him. That reason was unclear, but it definitely appeared to mean something to the killer. Secondly, Mr Jacob Stephenson, who was found suffocated by sweets being stuffed into his mouth. The coroner has confirmed that the sweets are all the same shape, oblong with ridges and rounded edges, but it's unclear what the actual sweet is or what it represents.'

'It looks like a little bug, or something,' Wayman spoke up. 'Which could be appropriate as he was in an allotment.'

'That's a good point,' Burton said, 'but what would the reason be for that? What is the murderer trying to say to us?' he asked the room as a whole, rather than directing the question back at Wayman. 'And thirdly,' he continued, getting back to his summary, 'Miss Dorothy Johnson, who had her head completely flattened by some sort of heavy wooden object.'

'It's turning into a game of Cluedo,' Francis declared, and if the whole situation wasn't so serious, it would have come across as a very amusing observation.

'And then we have two more murders up in the north east where Fielding is with Claire Rawlins today.' He nodded to Preston and another slide in the presentation appeared on the screen. 'On the right we have Jennifer Grayson, formerly Sanderson, and on the left Caroline Porter. These photos were taken a few years back and, strangely enough, Fielding used to go to school with them, as did Rawlins.'

Another nod from Burton and shots of their crime scenes popped up. 'As you can see, Grayson was beheaded and Porter was drowned.' The two photographs showed a very gruesome scene of Jennifer Grayson's decapitated body lying in a pool of blood with her head a short distance away, and one of Caroline Porter, head-deep in one of her water-filled plant pots. 'Again, a syringe mark was found at the base of the neck in the case of Caroline Porter, nothing for Jennifer Grayson, who we are assuming was beheaded from behind so there wasn't a need to sedate her. As with the other murders, a playing card was left at the scene of each crime. Plus, I've just had a call from Fielding up north telling me that both the victims up there were school governors, which seem to link both these murders to ours, even though they happened about two months ago and within a few days of one another.'

Another nod and two more images appeared.

'On the left, Alex Carruthers, great-nephew of Nathaniel Jackson, and on the right the unknown man, still not identified, who seemingly entered the care home under the guise of Carruthers to visit Jackson. At the present time,' Burton looked towards his DCI, 'Alex Carruthers is the only suspect that we have. At first we believed that he was his only relative, seeing as it was his name on the next of kin form at the home, and thought that he may have murdered his great-uncle for an inheritance.' A quick nod to Preston. 'But following Simon Banks's hospitalisation by a balaclava-wearing assailant at the scene of a break-in in Altrincham, it was discovered that the break-in took place at Nathaniel Jackson's old home, which is currently empty and up for sale. I investigated with DC Summers, and a window pane was broken in the back door, which must have been the point of entry, and a photograph was taken from a frame.

'The estate agent is currently trying to locate Jackson's other relatives and will be getting back to me as soon as they are found.' He paused for them to take it all in. 'We also have our profiler's take on this. Louise, would you care to come up to the front.' He indicated for her to come and take his place as he moved to an empty seat further back.

'Thank you, Detective Inspector Burton.' Louise Simmons stood before the screen but, not requiring the use of it, opened a folder she was holding instead. 'We appear to have two main links here, and they are education and the playing cards. These two things mean a lot to the killer and are very important to him – or them.'

Simmons looked around the room and continued, 'I say "them", as we really have two suspects here – Alex Carruthers and our John Doe, and if Carruthers is our main suspect, then he couldn't have committed the crimes in Manchester if he was up in the north east and vice versa. So if Carruthers is indeed behind all of these, then he must have had an accomplice to commit the crimes for him. This seems to be confirmed by the break-in in Altrincham where a photograph was taken from its frame. This says to me that the accomplice is on the photograph that was taken, and wishes to keep his identity a secret. Another fact about the cards revealed that they could symbolise education and the irresponsibility of youth – so if we take that as the basis for the crimes, then something happened to the killer when he was young, something to do with his education.'

'This seems to make perfect sense,' DCI Ambleton spoke up after hearing Burton and Simmons speak and taking this new information into account.

'There is one further factor in this, though,' Simmons revealed.

'And that is?' Ambleton asked of her.

'Now that we have all the information on the cases up in the north east, then Sally Fielding herself appears to be a link in all this.'

The room went silent.

Simmons continued, looking around her, 'Perhaps a case she has worked on over the years, something to do with her friends, even. I believe that, unbeknown to either us or her at this moment, she plays a part in this somewhere.'

It was then that Francis spoke up with a new take on this. 'You don't think that she's in any danger, do you?'

The DCI rolled this around in her head and spoke after giving it due consideration. 'We'll have to get someone to go through all her cases while she's been with us...'

'That will take forever, ma'am,' Burton intervened, but Ambleton had already considered that option.

'I know that you're not going to like this, Joe, but I'm going to get another team in to help us do the research on this one. Fielding has been with us how long now, almost ten years, and we just haven't got the manpower to go through every last little bit of it, so first thing Monday morning, I'll be enlisting more administrative help for this. And in answer to your question, DC Francis,' she added, turning to the young officer who had raised a very valid issue, 'I believe that to be a pertinent point, so I think it may be wise that we be extra vigilant and have Fielding's back on this one.'

19

'I really don't think that's necessary,' said Fielding when Burton told her.

Fielding wasn't ready for that when Burton rang her, but in some way after hearing of the connection between her two former school friends, she could understand how the profiler had arrived at that conclusion. Still, she didn't think it was necessary for anyone to stand guard over her, not that it had been suggested as yet, or for them to 'have her back'.

'What time are you getting home?' Burton had asked her, and when she told him that they were coming back earlier than expected and that she would be back at her apartment no later than seven, he'd asked her if she wanted to come over to his place and talk it over. With the promise of a takeaway, Fielding couldn't refuse the offer – even though they were supposed to be having time away from the investigation.

'But on one provision,' Fielding stipulated.

'What's that?' asked Burton.

'Just tone down the AC/DC volume, I don't want to be deafened like last time!'

He laughed. 'It's a deal. But you'll be pleased to know that I now wear headphones when I'm in the house!'

'Your neighbours threatening to complain to the police?' Fielding joked.

'Nearly, but not quite.'

* * *

Burton had to confess that a night off was exactly what the doctor had ordered, time to regroup and gather his wits about him and face the problem anew on Monday morning. He knew that there was a great deal to do, and although not happy at first about another team encroaching on his patch, the extra pairs of hands and eyes checking out Fielding's old cases would actually be a godsend.

Carruthers's questioning had reached a stalemate. He insisted that he knew nothing about any of the deaths. Burton believed that he somehow did, and was trying to push him so that he might slip up. By this time, Carruthers had had more than enough of 'this nonsense' as he'd adamantly put it. His solicitor had borne down on them and they'd had to reluctantly let him go. But in Burton's mind, he was far from out of the woods.

Following the meeting with Ambleton, he had gone down to see Carruthers, who had been his usual annoying self; and when shown the picture Burton had taken of his great-uncle's house and the row of photographs, Carruthers said that he couldn't remember what or who had been in the frame as he hadn't been in the house for a number of years. And Burton had to admit to himself that his response had seemed genuine enough. Carruthers had also confirmed who Nathaniel Jackson's other relatives were. The absence of a telephone call from the estate agent seemed to indicate that she hadn't been able to locate them.

Alex Carruthers's aunt and uncle, Jackson's son and daughter-in-law, lived in Brighton. Carruthers's own parents had retired to Spain some years back. Carruthers had not chosen to make the move with them because of the career he had formed for himself in this country. He was doing well here and didn't want to up sticks and try again in a foreign country. He also told Burton that he couldn't think of anyone who would want to murder his relative; he certainly had no reason to, or so he said, indicating that Jackson's son was the sole inheritor of his estate. That was something that Burton would have to check out for himself.

* * *

Burton's doorbell rang just before 7.45pm. *Good old Fielding,* he thought, *reliable as ever, always there when I need her.*

'What we having to eat then?' Fielding asked in a light-hearted way as soon as he answered the door for her.

'Can I open the door first and let you in!' Burton laughed as he opened his front door wider to enable her to enter.

'Sure you can. Now let me in, it's freezing out here!' She stamped both her feet up and down a few times, over-exaggerating her reaction to the cold. 'Oh, and I brought this with me,' she said, holding up a bottle of Prosecco. 'Maybe not your first choice of alcoholic beverage, but I couldn't fit a six-pack into my bag.'

'That'll do for me,' he told her, not wanting to admit that he'd already had two very welcome bottles of beer this evening.

Fielding handed him the bottle and slipped off her coat and hung it up on one of the pegs beside the front door, then walked through into the living room and sat herself down on the black leather sofa in front of the fire. The flickering flames of the log-effect gas fire were a very welcome sight, as was the heat they were giving off on such a bitterly cold night.

'Chinese or Indian?' Burton appeared from the kitchen holding up two takeaway menus, one in each hand.

'You choose, I'm good with either.'

They both decided on Chinese, and while Burton was ringing the order in, Fielding glanced around the room and caught sight of his dinner table. She couldn't remember a time when it didn't have anything on it – usually his laptop, phone, charger, a book, newspaper, magazine even, but she hadn't expected it to be as cluttered up as it was now with case files strewn all over it.

'I thought the DCI told us to take time off from this until Monday?' she asked when Burton reappeared from the kitchen carrying two plates and wine glasses.

'Well, I am having time off, Sal,' he said, walking over to her. She had already picked up one of the files, the one with Nathaniel Jackson's caseload in it, and was glancing through its contents. 'I haven't opened any of the files yet.' He put the plates and glasses down on an empty spot on the table then pointed to one of them. 'That's what the profiler has come up with so far; makes for interesting reading if you want to take a look at it.'

'So what you mean is you were waiting for me to come over before you started on them!' she joked, knowing full well that if that had been the reason, he would have just come out and asked.

'No, of course not!' He feigned hurt at such a suggestion. 'But… like I said, if you're already here…'

She threw one of his cushions at him.

Fielding should have known better than to expect Burton to completely switch off for the evening, and for the next day as well. He did relax, she knew that for a fact, but not usually when they were in the middle of a difficult case. That just wasn't his style, hers neither come to think of it. At least, as he'd said, he hadn't looked at the files yet, so that was a bit of a bonus. But he had intended to look at them, otherwise why bring them home in the first place? They had five murders on their hands, and to completely switch off and not think about them and leave things alone for a day and a half was not only unrealistic, but unprofessional. They couldn't be expected to just sit around not thinking about the case; that would have been impossible for them both. So she accepted the situation and agreed to go over everything again with him while waiting for the food to arrive.

20

'I just can't see any other answer than Carruthers being responsible.' Burton was draining the last of his Prosecco. The food had been delicious and Fielding's company was as welcome as ever. They were sitting going over the files again for the second time since they'd finished eating.

Fielding leaned back against the sofa. They were sitting on the floor in front of the fire surrounded by the case files, and she couldn't tell at this point if it was the Prosecco making her giddy or the contents of the files from over-reading them. As Burton had said, everything pointed to Carruthers – yet at the same time it did not.

'Contrariwise,' she said to herself more than to her colleague.

'What?' Burton was back on his feet now, heading towards the kitchen. She heard the fridge door open and close, and he returned with a can of beer in his hand. 'Want one?' he offered, thinking that perhaps he should have asked that when he was pulling one out of the pack for himself.

She shook her head; half a bottle of Prosecco was more than enough for her for the evening.

'What did you say before?' He sat down on the floor again beside her.

'Just a word that popped into my head from years ago. Don't know why it did after so long. How strange!'

'You'll have Louise Simmons analysing you if you're not careful,' he laughed, toying with the can in his hand.

'I think she already has, as she has concluded that I'm a link in this somehow,' she said pointing towards the files. 'Seriously, Joe, how can she think that I'm connected to this?'

'Well,' he popped the ring pull and took a long drink from the can, 'she's got that from your two school friends back home.'

She shook her head. 'I'm just not convinced, that's all.'

'Ambleton appears to think it a possibility, otherwise she would not be bringing in extra troops on Monday.'

'How do you feel about that?' Fielding asked, knowing full well that he took complete responsibility for all the cases he and the team were on and didn't like to be thought to be anything less than self-sufficient.

He just shrugged his shoulders and said, 'It can't hurt, I guess.' Adding, 'Now you're beginning to sound like a psychologist – "how do you feel?"'

'You know what I mean,' she insisted.

To which his response was, 'I know.'

After that, Fielding decided to call it a night and head back off home. Although going through the files had been interesting, she felt that she hadn't learned any more than she knew already, and besides, she felt she needed a break from it all as well as Burton did. So she called herself a taxi, thanked him for the takeaway, said good-night, gave him a peck on the cheek and headed off home to her cats and, hopefully, a good night's sleep.

* * *

Fielding may have been heading home to sleep, but Burton had other plans for the rest of the night. Pulling all-nighters weren't usually his style, as he, too, liked nothing more than to settle down in his warm, comfortable bed and drift off to a place as far away as possible from his job and all that it entailed. Unfortunately, that wasn't often the case. With the type of crimes they dealt with, the luxury of sweet dreams and a peaceful night's sleep was a nigh impossible thing to achieve, and he usually found himself tossing and turning most nights while trying to fight off every kind of assailant imaginable in the land of slumber. He didn't know if it was the combination of the Prosecco and the can of beer, but he felt wide awake and full of energy, raring to set to on the files again. There was something they were all missing here, and he was determined to find out what that was – even if it took him all night.

Despite all his good intentions, after only a few hours in, he felt his eyelids dropping. When the morning sun woke him up and he found himself slumped over the dining table surrounded by the files, one of which was sticking to his forehead, he was still without a definitive answer, other than all the evidence pointed to Alex Carruthers who, Burton had to confess, looked as guilty as hell.

* * *

Sally Fielding did exactly as she'd told Burton she was going to do. After leaving his apartment, she rode the taxi back to her place, fed her cats, watched a bit of inane so-called celebrity reality TV, then climbed into her bed and fell asleep.

Her dream was a strange one: she was younger, in her late teens, and walking in the small park near the home she grew up in. It was summer; the trees were full of life and colour, and the grass beneath her bare feet was a lush green. She could even feel it prickling her toes as she walked on it. As she rounded a corner, there were two children swinging in perfect synchronised movement in the play-ground area. They called out to her as she passed – but it wasn't her name they were calling, it was another name, one she couldn't quite catch.

She kept on walking until a bandstand appeared in view, decorated with multi-coloured bunting and balloons, and in the centre of the structure two elderly men were sitting playing chess, who stopped what they were doing to look up at her when she approached them. 'Hello, my name's Nate, what's yours?' the man in the clown outfit asked her. She was about to answer when the other man turned to her and opened his mouth to speak, but as he did, his mouth gaped open as far as it would go and what seemed like hundreds of beetles, earwigs and millipedes all came spewing out of it.

It was at that point that Fielding awoke with a start, and in a cold sweat – or she thought that she was in a cold sweat and that her wet face was due to the after effects of the nightmarish dream, but then she realised that she had a cat sitting on either side of her head, each licking her face with a sense of urgency.

Glancing at the clock, she saw that it was just after ten. No wonder they were frantic, as she was always an early morning riser and they should have enjoyed their breakfast long before now, then settled down on their cat beds for their post-breakfast nap.

'Okay, okay,' she laughed, brushing them away from her face. With a quick meow apiece, they scuttled away out of the bedroom and into the kitchen, and sat expectantly around their bowls waiting for food.

After giving them their breakfast, she decided to skip hers and go out for a jog before lunch. She'd always enjoyed a run on a weekend when she wasn't working, but the last few months had put paid to that as the workload had been much greater than usual with everyone being required to do extra shifts just to cope with it all. So her once-regular routine had faded into non-existence.

Then she'd bought herself a tracker watch in the summer and had been determined to put it to good use when the level of work had died down. This was the first real chance she'd had to put it to its proper use, even though she wore it on a daily basis, plus she felt she had to run off the previous night's Chinese meal at Burton's... and the half bottle of Prosecco that she'd drunk with him while eating it, as both were now weighing heavily on her stomach... and her head.

So she delved into her wardrobe and dug out a pair of exercise leggings and top, together with a hoodie, then slipped on her trainers from the shoe rack beside the front door and ventured out on to a route she used to regularly run, which took her into and around Heaton Park.

The huge 600 acre historic area on the edge of Manchester was a big drawing point in the summer with a full range of attractions including play areas, cafés, an animal centre, a tram museum, bowling greens, golf course and a boating lake.

During the autumn and winter months, it was mostly a place where joggers and dog walkers could be found, rather than the seasonal tourists and sightseers who enjoyed the peace and quiet of the very wide and very open space to themselves.

Fielding was halfway around the boating lake when she realised just how close she was to the care home where Nathaniel Jackson had died, which in turn made her think about the case. She sighed. *I'd hoped a jog would stop me thinking about the case, not bring it to the fore.* She stopped by a bench and sat down on it, pressing the side button on her watch to check the number of steps she'd done. Ten thousand already... not bad.

Thoughts of the care home led her in turn to think about the murders of her two school friends back on Tyneside. Although they'd all been very close back in the day, inseparable in fact, all that had been thirteen years ago and a lot could happen in that length of time. In her case, she had moved away from the area and cut all ties to her previous existence, and that had all been down to her mother's and sister's reaction to her choice of career.

But why hadn't she kept in touch with her best friends? In some ways she felt ashamed by that, but on the other hand, people change, they go off and lead completely separate and different lives, and simply drift apart. If she had stayed, if she had remained in Boldon and still been close to them, might she have ended up as one of the victims as well? She tried her best to imagine what they could possibly have had in common which led to them being victims of a serial killer – for victims of a serial killer they most definitely were, together with the three victims here in Manchester. What was it that connected two of her former school mates with three elderly people here in the city?

The education link was now apparent with the revelation that both Jennifer and Caroline were school governors. But could it simply be, as profiler Louise Simmons had suggested, a case of one intended victim with others as red herrings?

Her head was now spinning; a combination of the crisp, fresh autumnal air blowing away the cobwebs, the 10,000 steps on her pedometer, hunger despite overeating the previous evening, the half bottle of wine and the complexity of the case. Deciding that the jog hadn't exactly been the distraction that she'd needed, she decided to call it a day and head home again. She would spend the rest of the day curled up in front of the television with her cats likewise curled up next to her.

21

By the time Burton got into work on Monday morning, two official forms were sitting on his desk in the office. The first one was confirming the deployment of a group of five admin staff and two detective constables from the neighbouring Salford division into his. He was required to sign off on it and return to DCI Ambleton as soon as possible. He stood up and looked through his office window and saw that the admin staff were already seated around the room at the spare desks and busy at work. *Very efficient,* he thought.

The second form was a request that he contact a DC James Morrison, who was part of the household crime division on the second floor. He picked up his phone and dialled the number provided. DC Morrison answered almost immediately.

'Ah yes, sir,' he said after hearing who the caller was. Burton could hear papers rustling on the other end of the phone and visualised Morrison shuffling his documents around trying to find his copy of the form... and then success. 'Here we are, there was a theft in the city yesterday, which I attended, and when I entered the name of the victim into the system, it came up as being linked to a case of yours. I just thought that I would make you aware, sir, just in case it was relevant to your case.'

Now extremely curious as to who it might be, Burton asked him for the name of the person and was more than a little surprised to hear it was Monica Williams, who, he remembered, was Alex Carruthers's next-door neighbour. He'd spoken to her just the other day. 'Exactly what happened?' Burton asked him, thinking that this couldn't possibly be a coincidence.

'She had been out to the cinema with a friend and when she returned at around 2.30pm, she found that her apartment had been broken into. Although the door was closed, the lock had been broken along with the door frame and when she looked around, all that was missing was her phone,' Morrison explained.

'You mean that she didn't have it with her?' Burton found that difficult to comprehend in this day and age, but then remembered that when he and Fielding had been to see her, she'd had to retrieve her phone from the sideboard to find them a photograph of Alex Carruthers.

'I know,' Morrison told him, 'it is unusual, but she said that she rarely uses it and only mainly for taking photographs. Also, she was at the cinema and she says it wasn't necessary. I just wish more people were like her, don't you?'

Burton admitted that he did. He couldn't keep track of the number of accidents caused by people having their eyes permanently stuck on the screen of their mobile phones. He thanked Morrison for his diligence and then shouted through for Fielding to come into the office.

'Yes, sir,' she said, opening the door and sticking her head through it.

'We're going out on a little trip to see Alex Carruthers's neighbour again.' And seeing her questioning look, he explained the events of the previous day.

* * *

'I just can't believe that somebody broke in and only stole my phone. I'd like to think that I've got things of more value in the house than that!' Monica Williams joked as she showed them into her living room once again. Apart from the noticeable wear and tear on the door frame indicating that someone had forced their way in and entered illegally, nothing had changed in her apartment. It was still orderly and well-kept, and anyone with a compulsion for keeping things clean would have nothing to worry about in here as it was virtually spotless.

Burton and Fielding sat down on her very comfortable sofa as she continued. 'But it's strange, isn't it, someone stealing my phone after I'd just shown you that photo the other night?'

'Just what we were thinking, Miss Williams,' Fielding told her. 'In fact, that's why we've come back.'

'Oh please,' she insisted, 'do call me Monica.'

'Tell me, Miss... Monica...' Burton began, 'you do have a backup storage system of some kind though, don't you?' He was sincerely hoping that this was the case.

'Yes, I do have cloud backup, but everything has been wiped from it. I just checked on my laptop this morning.'

Both Burton's and Fielding's hearts sank on hearing that. The phone was obviously connected to their enquiry, otherwise why would it have been stolen and the backup storage deleted. There again, Carruthers was centre stage, right at the front of everything – he was a computer whizz-kid after all, travelling around the country with his job, setting up businesses with their computer systems and showing them how to use them.

'However,' Monica Williams said, seeing the looks on their faces, 'I do have copies of everything I photograph.'

The two detectives exchanged glances with one another and she continued, 'I have an external hard drive that I put everything on after I've taken photos.'

'So everything that you had on the phone will be on there?' Fielding asked, and she nodded confirmation.

'Would you like me to upload everything onto a flash drive?'

'If you wouldn't mind,' Burton said, feeling extremely grateful that her orderly nature seemed to apply to everything.

* * *

'You know,' Fielding said to Burton when they were back at the station and seated in his office working their way through all of Monica Williams's massive collection of photographs, 'what's to say Carruthers didn't alter the records at his place of employment up in the north east?'

Burton took his eyes from his computer screen and considered the question. It was something that he had been rolling around in his mind for a couple of days now, but, there again, there was no proof whatsoever to back this theory up. How could there be with a tech wizard calling all the shots, if indeed he was calling them, as any footprint would be wiped into oblivion. And another thing that had crossed Burton's mind was the fact that Carruthers could have easily intercepted their dispatch messages if he'd wanted to. Perhaps all this was sufficient grounds to bring a charge against him after all: bring him in, get a hold of his computer and get forensics to take it to pieces to get an in-depth look at it.

Hell, he could have even been the unknown John Doe at the care home if he'd changed his appearance to suit the situation. He remembered that he'd said in passing that the unknown man could have easily been mistaken for Carruthers as he looked so much like him. Maybe, in fact, it was him.

'How far back should we go with all of these?' Fielding had just passed the 500-photo mark and looked up from the laptop perched on her knees, eyes beginning to smart from focusing so hard on each of the images. The question brought Burton out of his thoughts with a start.

'As far back as we need to, I guess,' he offered, realising that his answer wouldn't really help her in any way and wasn't what she wanted to hear. 'I'm just wondering about that friend of Carruthers's, who Monica Williams said was camera-shy. Maybe he had a good reason to be.'

At that moment, Burton's desk phone rang and he picked it up. He said a few monosyllabic words in response to questions he was being asked, then replaced the receiver.

'The boss wants me to go upstairs and give her an update. Can you keep going through this lot?' He indicated that Fielding should continue working her way through the photo file on her laptop. 'If we look for anyone who looks like Carruthers,' he suggested, seeing the look of frustration on her face, 'I get the feeling that our John Doe might just know him.'

* * *

'Do you think we have enough to charge him?' DCI Ambleton asked after hearing Burton relate everything they had on the case so far.

He exhaled a long breath. 'We have plenty against him, it's just...' his voice trailed off.

'What's bothering you, Joe?' Ambleton sat back in her chair. She could see that despite all the incriminating evidence building up against Alex Carruthers, which she would be happy to book him on right now, Burton was still troubled by something.

'It just doesn't feel right somehow, boss.'

'In what way?' She waited for him to explain his reasoning behind the statement.

'It just seems too obvious that it's him. I spent Saturday night going through the files with Fielding, and...'

'I thought I told you to take some time off, you and Fielding,' the DCI said, showing annoyance at what he'd just told her. 'I can't have my detectives burnt out and running on half-empty now, can I?'

'I know, I know,' Burton insisted, holding both his hands up in surrender, 'but this... there's something not quite right about it. There's something that we're missing here.'

The DCI thought about that before answering. 'Well, you know sometimes these people who commit crimes slip up, or even want to be caught.'

There was silence between them for a few moments before Ambleton responded to his doubts with an option.

'Okay. Look, Joe, I think that we can bring the man in for questioning with what we have right now and hold him for thirty-six hours before charging him for the crime, and if you aren't happy and have doubts, then I'm all right with you doing some more digging. But, officially, I'm going to go ahead and close it down after the thirty-six hours. At least that will keep the press off our backs if we say we have a suspect with an arrest pending while we look into it a bit more.'

22

After being questioned a few days earlier, Alex Carruthers had been told not to travel up to the north east to his work after the weekend, and when Burton and Fielding had pressed the buzzer for his apartment on the building's intercom system, they were surprised yet delighted to find him at home. As per the DCI's instructions, they had come to officially take him in for questioning, and they weren't alone as two uniformed police officers stood behind them.

'Is this really necessary?' Carruthers said when told by Burton what was about to happen. 'I said I wouldn't go up north today and I haven't.'

'Yes, it is necessary,' Fielding assured him. 'And we are taking you in for questioning about the murder of your great-uncle.'

Amid a flurry of protestations, Carruthers was taken by each arm by the uniforms and marched unceremoniously out of his apartment, much to his embarrassment, especially as a few of his neighbours opened their doors to find out what all the raised voices and commotion was about.

'Can I not even call my solicitor?' he had demanded when seated in the back of the police car, wedged securely yet uncomfortably between the two uniformed officers.

'You can do that when you get to the station... now shut up!' Burton's voice was as firm as his expression as he looked at him in the rear-view mirror. Then, turning around to face the road, Burton concentrated on driving him back there as soon as he could.

* * *

Basil Mowbray was one of those obnoxious little solicitors with clammy hands and slicked back greasy hair who was only in the legal profession for one thing – himself. For him it was all about what he could get out of it, whether that was money, fame, publicity, whatever, as long as the sole attention was on him and his success, and never on his client. Nasty little man and, as fate would have it, Alex Carruthers's regular solicitor was unavailable and he was now stuck with this vile creature. Carruthers was up in arms, but there was nothing he could do.

Mowbray read through his client's file as they sat in one of the interview rooms. His face was expressionless and he said nothing until he'd reached the last page and closed the manila folder. 'Well,' he said, looking to Carruthers on his right and the two detectives across the table from him, 'I can't see how you can hold my client on this.' He spat the last word out with disdain and pushed the folder across the table to them. 'Tell me, detectives, exactly where is your evidence that this man sitting here,' indicating Carruthers with a sweep of his hand, 'is anything other than innocent of the charges you've brought against him?'

Burton had dealt with the creep before and had expected exactly this from him.

Fielding, on the other hand, had not had the dubious pleasure of his company, but Burton had briefed her well on what he was like.

She had to admit that his description of him was spot on. She had decided before even making his acquaintance that she didn't like him; truth was, nobody but the man himself liked him, not even the partners in the company he worked for.

'Well, like it or not, Mr Mowbray,' Burton said, picking up the folder and rising from his seat, gesturing for his partner to do likewise, 'we are holding your client for the next thirty-six hours and there is absolutely nothing you can do about it.'

'But I insist upon bail,' he started to protest.

But Burton cut him off with, 'Not a chance,' as he and Fielding walked out of the room and closed the door behind them.

* * *

'Mowbray is spitting blood,' DCI Ambleton said on the phone following the detectives' return to the incident room. 'I thought he was going to have a coronary. The man was almost purple by the time he came in to see me in my office.'

'Well, let him,' Burton retorted. 'That man thinks far too highly of himself for his own good.'

'Now, Joe, you know that, and I know that, but we don't want to fall foul of the law now, do we?'

'That's a bit ironic, isn't it?'

DCI Ambleton sighed and waited for a few moments. 'All right then, we now have Carruthers in custody. You've got your thirty-six hours to do any extra research you need, Joe. Make sure you use that time wisely.'

'Oh we will, don't worry, boss.' Burton put the phone back on the receiver and sat back in his chair. With Alex Carruthers tucked up nicely in the cells for the next day and a half, he, Fielding and the team would have time to go through the photographs and anything else they needed to before releasing him. But as far as the press knew, they'd already made an arrest and Carruthers would be standing trial. It would no doubt end up like that, unless they found anything to prove to the contrary.

Burton admitted he disliked Carruthers, but the last thing he wanted was to charge an innocent man with a crime he hadn't committed, no matter how much he despised him. That wasn't what he was about, and he would do what he had to to get to the truth of any matter. He was still deep in thought when Fielding rapped a couple of times on the door.

'I think you should come and see this,' she said, turning quickly to lead the way back to her computer monitor. She sat down and tapped her password into the system. A photograph sprung to life on the screen. 'You see that person there?' she said, pointing to someone standing at the back of the photograph. It was date stamped 'August' and showed a group of four people in Monica Williams's apartment. It had been taken by somebody other than Monica herself as she was in the centre of the shot. Apart from her, there was another woman, another man and Carruthers. But what Fielding was pointing to was the man standing in the back beside the kitchen breakfast bar, seemingly oblivious to the fact that he was being captured on camera. She lifted up the sketch artist's shot of their John Doe and held it up against the monitor.

'I think,' she said excitedly, 'that if you were to add hair on that face, then it could quite easily be the man we've been looking for.'

Burton leaned in closer and looked from the face on the screen to the artist's drawing and had to admit that the features were as close as you could get. 'Can we get that blown up,' he asked, 'without losing any definition?'

'I'll certainly try,' she told him. 'And if I can't, then I'm sure our tech team can do something about that.'

Seeing the activity around Fielding's computer screen, DC Francis came across to see what they were looking at, closely followed by Wayman.

'Have we struck lucky?' Francis asked, looking at the screen.

'Well I certainly hope so,' Burton told her.

'I thought Carruthers said that he didn't recognise the person in the sketch?' Wayman quite rightly observed.

'That he did, Sam, that he did.'

Before going down to the cells to have a word with Carruthers, Burton first checked with the desk sergeant to make sure that Basil Mowbray had definitely left the building. He hadn't wished to bump into him again today, or any other day come to that, and was delighted to hear that he had signed out and left the premises about half an hour ago. The desk sergeant added that he hadn't left quietly, saying that he intended to lodge an official written complaint with the chief constable as soon as he got back to his practice and found some headed notepaper – something which Burton didn't doubt for a second.

Carruthers looked at the photograph. 'I met him on a computer course a few months back.' Fielding had successfully enlarged it to give a clear image of the man's face. 'I tutor groups on government-sponsored courses, and that was where I met Jim.'

'Jim?' Burton asked, pen perched ready over his notebook.

'Yes, Jim Martindale. He'd signed up for a four-week refresher course in programming. He was a good student, we got on well, had quite a few things in common, and we became friends. Just one of those things, I guess.'

'There'd be an address for him on record, I imagine?' Fielding asked, feeling that this information was proving to be a huge step forward in the case.

'Oh yes, of course, the centre the course was held in will have all that.'

'You didn't visit his home address?' Burton paused from his writing.

'No, he said that he still lived with his parents and that there really wasn't any room to entertain any friends.'

Burton and Fielding exchanged curious glances, but Fielding posed the question both on their minds. 'Were you in a relationship with Mr Martindale?'

'What?' Carruthers appeared genuinely shocked by that comment.

Fielding remembered what she'd been told by the manager of ComputerLinks, that he was always a great hit with the female members of staff. But that could have all been a front for his real preferences of course.

However, Carruthers dispelled that thought in his next sentence. 'No... of course not... I'm not gay, never have been, never will be. How can you possibly think that?'

'Well, we're just trying to cover all options,' Burton tried to calm him down as he could see that this was going to go south fairly quickly if he didn't say anything – and they were making very good progress so far.

'I did invite him around to my apartment a couple of times – just as a friend, I'll have you know.' Carruthers stared at both of them with a look of disgust. 'And on a couple of those occasions, we did go around to Monica's flat as she was having one of her arty dos.'

'One of her arty dos?' Fielding asked him, unsure what he meant by that.

'Well, she's an artist and photographer, and mixes with a lot of the arty set, like other photographers and artists and such. Told me she even has a studio set-up in her second bedroom. She's a very social person from what I can gather, and likes to entertain – not noisily you understand, as I've never had anything to complain about in that respect. I think that she invited me as I gave her some computer advice a while back. She knew that I lived on my own, and I suppose she was trying to introduce me to some of her friends.'

When Burton asked him what sort of computer advice he gave her, Carruthers explained that she needed more storage for her massive photograph collection and he'd suggested that she buy an external hard drive to store them on. Had even shown her how to transfer files and back them up.

23

Back in his office, Burton slumped down in his chair and Fielding sat on the seat across the desk from him.

'That was unexpected,' he said, trying to get to grips with what he'd just been told.

'That would seem to put him in the clear, wouldn't it?'

'If we can believe what he said.' Burton looked at her with doubting eyes. He both wanted to believe the man and also not believe him at the same time. But he knew that they needed to contact the training centre where Jim Martindale had studied under Alex Carruthers's tutorage and find out where he lived. That task was given to DC Wayman.

While DC Wayman was busily at work on the telephone, Fielding could hear her phone ringing back on her desk. The caller display told her it was Claire Rawlins calling her. She hadn't expected another call from her so soon.

'Hi, Claire,' she said. 'What can I do for you?'

'I was wondering,' Rawlins began, 'if you'd like to come over to my place this evening? I've been recalled back up to my work in the north east and I'm not sure when I'll get the chance to meet up with you again, as I can't see you heading back up there anytime soon.' She laughed gently. 'I heard that you've arrested somebody in the murder cases, so I'm hoping that you'd be free. Please say yes!'

Claire didn't seem to realise that working in the police force wasn't a nine-to-five job. Maybe she could clock off work when the little hand on the clock struck the number five, but that wasn't the case with everyone. However, Fielding took a moment to consider the situation. With Carruthers waiting in the cells pending an official arrest in thirty-six hours' time, they had to move quickly to find the man they now knew as Jim Martindale, and bring him in for questioning. But maybe Burton would let her off on that one and take a detective constable with him when he went to get Martindale. 'Give me a moment,' Fielding said and cupped the phone while she went and asked Burton if that option was a possibility.

'Why not... yes, go on, take the night off and I'll see you bright and early in the morning.' He seemed more upbeat than he'd been a short while ago, and a million miles away from the man who had taken care of the greasy solicitor with his harsh tongue and firm stance. Perhaps he could see the light at the end of the tunnel, and that was something they all definitely needed right now.

But, back to the phone call.

'Yes, Claire, that's fine,' she told her when she'd had Burton's go-ahead. 'Just text me the address and time and I'll see you then.'

'That's great, I'll send you the information now... and I'm really looking forward to seeing you again.' And true to her word, a few minutes later the text message containing her temporary address in the city was delivered with a ping to Fielding's phone.

Fielding was packing up her desk for the night when DC Summers got up from his desk. He went sprinting across the room to Burton's office and rapped urgently on the closed door. She saw Burton indicate for him to go in. Then both of them emerged within seconds and headed back towards Summers's desk.

'What's going on?' Fielding asked.

'They've found Jim Martindale's address,' said Burton, excitement showing in his voice. 'Okay, Summers, Wayman, I want both of you to come with me on this one, just in case he decides to do a runner when we get there. Summers, you're a lot fitter and younger than me and Wayman.'

The three detectives collected what they needed and left the office in full flight, creating something of a whirlwind in their wake. Fielding watched as they disappeared then continued tidying up her workstation. When she'd finished, she said goodnight to the two remaining DCs and the admin staff, then headed home to her two cats before getting ready for her evening out with Claire Rawlins.

Jim Martindale's address was in the Hulme area of Manchester. Burton and his team noticed that there was already a vehicle parked up on the driveway. He was home, or at least somebody was, as they didn't know whether he lived alone, with a friend or partner, or if he lived with his parents even. Burton directed Summers to go around the back of the house and Wayman to stand by the side gate, which appeared to go to the rear garden. He approached the front door himself and tried the doorbell. Through the crinkled glass of the half-paned door, he saw a light go on in the hallway, then a figure walked towards the door.

'Yes? Who is it?' a male voice called out. Clearly he did not wish to open the door until he knew who was there.

'It's the police, sir,' Burton announced, 'and we are trying to locate a Mr Jim Martindale. Is that you?'

There was the sound of a chain being removed. Then the door opened to reveal a middle-aged man standing there. Burton showed him his warrant card. 'Jim? No, that's not me... it's my son. What's happened? Is he all right?'

'We're just trying to speak to him with regard to a course he was on recently.'

'A course? What kind of course?' the man asked, seeming confused by the whole line of questioning.

Burton told him that it was a computer one.

'I don't understand,' Mr Martindale senior stated, now more than slightly annoyed. 'My son wouldn't be on a computer course.'

'How could you be so sure, sir?' Burton had been patient with the man so far, but was now becoming irritated by him. 'If we could just have a quick word with–'

But he was cut off mid-sentence.

'I'd like to see you try,' the boy's father declared sharply, finally fed up with the police officer and his questions. 'You couldn't do anything for him when it happened, so go ahead, try to get him to speak to you.'

'I don't understand,' Burton was confused.

'Try the Royal Infirmary,' he said sharply. 'He's been in there in a coma since he was knocked down last year. Your people still haven't found out who did it.'

Burton was shocked – and speechless. He hadn't expected that. He hadn't stopped to check the name out before rushing out with his team with all guns blazing. He should at least have put the name of Jim Martindale through their systems. It would have shown up as being the victim of a hit-and-run, as this had seemed to be. He brought the photograph out of his pocket and showed it to Mr Martindale senior.

Shaking his head, he said, 'I've no idea who this person is, I've never seen him before in my life. Does that mean that you will now investigate my boy's accident properly?' The father looked him straight in the eyes, full of hope and desperate for an affirmation. He must have spent the last year waiting for somebody from the police force to come knocking on his door to tell him that the perpetrator had finally been found and charged. And here was Burton, rolling up without so much as doing a background check, and landing on his doorstep full of ignorance and bad preparation.

Burton floundered, now not knowing what to tell the man. The delay did not go unnoticed.

'Right,' Mr Martindale senior said, 'I won't hold my breath,' and slammed the door in his face.

24

It was quite a change for Fielding to put on a bit of make-up, spray some perfume on her wrists, pick out a smart evening outfit, a pair of heeled shoes way too high to wear for everyday work and spend an evening away from the cats and the TV.

She pressed the bell and waited for Claire to come and let her in, holding the bottle of wine that she'd brought with her. She didn't have much of an inkling of what sort of wine Claire preferred, but had chosen a bottle of sparkling rosé. It really went with anything and everything, and how could she go wrong with that? Claire hadn't said if they were staying in or going out, but whatever it was going to be, a glass of the bubbly would set them up.

'Come in, come in,' Claire greeted her warmly and opened the door wide for her to enter.

As she walked into the hallway, Fielding glanced around her, taking note of her whereabouts and taking everything into account. *A hazard of the job,* she thought.

Claire must have read her thoughts as she said, 'You can have a night off once in a while, you know!'

Fielding laughed. 'Am I that obvious?' she said, 'A police officer twenty-four-seven.'

'Just a bit.' Claire took her coat and hung it up on the coat rack beside a long, oak-coloured console table with an ornate mirror positioned centrally above it.

She said, 'I'm surprised that you haven't got your notebook out to jot everything down.'

'No, that's Burton's thing, not mine.' Fielding could see him in her mind, reaching for that book inside his jacket.

'Come on, let's go and sit down.' Claire Rawlins led her into a lovely front room, halfway between modern and traditional, with a realistic-looking gas fire on the chimney breast stealing the focal point and directing the eyes towards it. The heat it was giving off was very welcome, and in stark contrast to the crisp evening air outside. Again, like the mirror above the console table in the hallway, there was an equally elegant and unusual one above the mantelpiece. Almost the full width of the chimney breast and about half the height, the oblong mirror was surrounded by what looked like a mosaic of small, irregular pieces of reflective glass. The effect of the light bouncing off them was intriguing.

'Would you like me to open this now?' Claire said, holding up the bottle of rosé Fielding had handed to her on the way in. Fielding nodded. It had been sitting in her fridge for a few weeks, so it was well and truly chilled.

'Make yourself comfortable and I'll just go and pour this for us.' Claire held up the bottle and smiled, indicating for Fielding to sit down on one of the two large cream sofas while she headed off to the kitchen in search of glasses. Fielding did as she was told and sat facing the fire. It felt as if she was sinking into the comfort of the memory foam, it was so soft yet supportive. It was the luxury her old sofa lacked – too many years sitting on the same part of it had flattened it to the point where it was a shadow of its former self. Perhaps she should invest in a new one soon.

'Here we go,' Claire announced, coming in holding two almost full glasses of the pink fizz, and handing one over to Fielding. 'Cheers,' she said, and they both took a sip.

They still had a lot to catch up with. They'd briefly gelled again on the trip up to the north east, but thirteen years of catching up cannot be covered in the space of a day. It was good to speak to someone from back in the old days.

Claire Rawlins had come to her school in the last two years she'd attended. Her family had moved to Boldon from further up in Northumberland. Claire's father had taken a job as a consultant dermatologist at the Royal Victoria Infirmary in Newcastle city centre, and she had said then that she'd planned to follow in his footsteps and go into medicine.

As Fielding had left the north east immediately after getting the results of her A-levels, she never knew whether that ambition had been fulfilled or not. That in turn made her consider the lives of Jennifer Grayson and Caroline Porter. What had they done after they'd left school? Had something they'd both been involved with led to their murders.

'Penny for them?' Claire laughed, bringing Fielding out of her thoughts.

'I'm so sorry, Claire,' she told her friend. 'It's this case, it's been on my mind so much that I just can't seem to relax. You know, I even went out jogging the other day and had to quit halfway through as I couldn't stop thinking about it. It didn't help that I was in the park just next to where the first victim here died.'

'I know just what you mean,' Claire told her. 'Sometimes I get a case come in that I feel I need to know more about, not just the dissecting end of it.'

'Nice!' Fielding laughed, conjuring up a grotesque image of Rawlins bent over a slab cutting up dead bodies all day long.

'But you've found the killer now, haven't you?' Claire took a long sip of wine.

Not really wanting to disclose too much about the case, even to someone that she knew, Fielding simply told her that they had made an arrest. She didn't need to know right now that they were still trying to find somebody else linked to the case. Nobody did until they'd found Jim Martindale, questioned him and, if need be, arrested him.

'Then relax, Sally, you can afford to take the night off from this. Tell me,' she continued, changing the subject, 'what about that dishy DI that you work with?'

Fielding looked at her quizzically, 'You mean Burton? Joe?'

'Yes, Joe Burton... is he single?'

'Are you after him then?'

Claire smiled. 'No, not me. I was thinking about you. You two just friends, or more than that?'

'We're friends, we're colleagues... and that's it. Why do you ask?'

'I just thought that I saw a connection there.' Claire put her glass down on the side table.

'Well of course you would, Claire. We've been partners now for about seven years; you get to know somebody well in that time. And you come to depend upon them.'

'Okay, okay,' Claire laughed, hands up in the air in defence.

Having got that off her chest, Claire changed the line of conversation, and with it the mood. 'Music?' she said, rising up from the sofa and moving over towards the CD system on the shelf just to the right of the fireplace. She looked through the collection of CDs beneath it and, finding one she liked the look of, popped it out of its case and into the drawer of the player. They talked about their school days to a background of seventies music, then about what they had been doing in the years that had followed.

Claire had indeed gone straight into medicine, studied at Newcastle University, then gone to work at the coroner's office in North Tyneside.

Sally talked about her reasons for moving to Manchester.

'No chance of a reconciliation then?' Claire asked.

Fielding shook her head, wondering if her old school friend had not got the message from her previous response to this line of questioning. 'I think too much time has passed now for any of us to make the first move. Maybe it's for the best.'

They talked more about life back in the north east, about people they'd been to school with, where they might be now, based on what they were like then. Fielding even speculated who, in her humble opinion as a police officer, may even be in prison now. Claire thought that last observation amusing, and very probably correct. Fielding realised that they had been talking for quite some time now and, glancing discreetly at her watch, saw that it was just past half eight.

It occurred to her that she hadn't eaten since lunchtime. Was that why she was feeling so light-headed?

'More wine?' Claire already had both their glasses in her hands.

25

B ack at the station, Burton stood in front of the cork board looking at the photograph of Jim Martindale.

Where do we go from here? he wondered. The only thing was to get this photograph circulated as soon as possible. A real photograph was far better than a sketch artist's image. And that meant going to the media again.

It was now fast approaching six o'clock and half of his team would be signing off their shift for the night. Fielding had already left for her evening out at Claire Rawlins's house, and he was delighted that she was getting time away from this case. But it looked as if he and Wayman would be making a few phone calls before they left for the night.

DC Francis was just closing her computer down when her fiancé, Sean Dylan, appeared in the doorway and waved. He worked on the dispatch team and on the very rare occasions that they shared the same shift end time, he would come down from the third floor and they'd drive home together.

'Hi, Sean,' Burton called across to him when he saw him standing there. 'At least some of us are getting home early tonight.'

'Yes, and both at the same time too. Doesn't often work out that way.'

Burton laughed. 'That's so true.' Then waved him in, 'Come on in, you needn't stand on ceremony in the doorway.'

'Thanks.' He moved across to Jane Francis's desk and gave her a quick peck on the cheek.

'I won't be long,' she said, putting her files away in the drawers and locking them up before hanging up the key in the small wall safe at the back of the room along with all the other desk keys.

As Sean's eyes wandered around the room, they landed on the cork board Burton was standing in front of. 'Oh,' he said, walking over to it. 'Why is there a photograph of Rob Pratchett on there?'

Burton spun around and saw Sean's eyes firmly on the photograph of their John Doe.

'What?' he asked incredulously, hardly able to get his breath. 'You know this person?' Hearing this, the other officers and admin staff left in the room all stopped what they were doing in unison and looked towards him. Francis came up and stood beside him.

Sean looked around, conscious that all eyes were now on him, and discovering that they were. 'Yes,' he said after a brief pause. 'It's Rob. He's one of the dispatchers upstairs... or should I say, he was, he left last Friday. Going back up north, or something like that, he said.' Turning to Francis, he said, 'You know that do I went to on Friday evening? It was for him leaving.'

Burton had heard DC Francis say on so many occasions how great Sean was with anything to do with computers and tech, so he asked whether Rob Pratchett was likewise proficient in the skill.

'Is he ever!' Sean said in sheer admiration. 'The man's an absolute genius when it comes to computers. Did you know he's also a member of MENSA?'

Burton had already heard enough. 'Wayman,' he shouted, 'get upstairs quickly and find his home address.'

'What's going on?' Sean asked, confused by Burton's excitement at his revelation. 'Is he in some kind of trouble?'

'I think you've just cracked our case wide open.' Burton could have kissed the man.

* * *

'I don't think I should have any more after this, Claire,' said Fielding, her voice sounding just a little bit off as she said it. 'It's gone to my head. Maybe we should eat something now.'

At that moment, the song on the CD changed to something that Fielding hadn't heard in a very long time, right back to the time she was in secondary school. It was one of her favourites, as she recalled, back in the day, as it reminded her so much of her all-time favourite book. *One pill makes you larger, and one pill makes you small* the woman's voice was singing, and the image of a white rabbit sprang immediately into her head. 'Oooooh,' she declared, 'I haven't heard this song for ages.' Fielding heard her voice almost slur the sentence.

'I know,' Claire told her, her voice sounding as if it was coming from some way off.

'Claire... I don't feel right...' she managed to get a few words out before she couldn't speak any more.

Then the song seemed to go out of tune. In fact, it was at that point that she herself seemed to go out of tune. The mirror above the mantelpiece again caught her attention as the mosaic pieces of reflective glass surrounding it seemed to break away and swirl around in front of her, light bouncing off each piece to create a kaleidoscope of patterns and shapes. She looked across at Claire, who was staring directly at her. Her mouth was moving and she seemed to be saying something to her but she couldn't make out what it was. The music distorted even more *And your mind is moving low* – that's exactly how it felt for her right now, her mind was moving low, slowing down, even Claire rising from her seat opposite was choreographed in slow motion and not at normal speed. *What is happening? Why am I feeling like this?*

Then she heard another voice in the room. 'Is she going under?' A man's voice, far off in the distance, as if down a long tunnel, distorted.

Who is this, and who is going under? wondered Fielding.

Claire said, 'Yes she is,' and moved away from the sofa to be replaced by a man. Or at least Fielding thought it to be a man. The face alternated between a man's head and that of a large rabbit, wavering in and out of focus.

Or is it my eyes wavering in and out of focus? Fielding couldn't be sure. She couldn't be certain of anything right now.

It was as if she was on some weird, drug-induced psychedelic trip. But every few seconds, when the morphing features solidified into that of a man, she stared at him, trying to recognise him. Then she realised, in those last few moments of consciousness, that she was looking at the face of their John Doe. She tried to speak but was unable to as her mouth wouldn't respond to her instructions.

'Time to go down the rabbit hole, Alice,' he said, his voice echoing harshly in her head.

She felt herself falling sideways onto the sofa from her upright position. *Alice? Nobody has called me that since I was at school.* She tried to explain, 'I use my middle name, Sally, now...' But darkness took over.

26

DC Wayman didn't even wait for the lift but sprinted up the two flights of stairs to the contact centre.

All eyes were on him as he ran through the desks to the main office at the back of the room, but his speed was so great that nobody there had time to rise up and challenge his odd behaviour. All he left in his wake was unanswered questions and shocked expressions.

The supervisor sitting behind the desk was taken by surprise when he flung the door open and came to a stop at its edge, slapping both hands flat on the desk.

'What the...' the supervisor, whose badge indicated her name to be Ingrid, began. But Wayman cut her off to explain the situation and what he and the rest of his team needed from her... right now.

Burton paced the floor waiting for his DC to return, shocked by what Jane Francis's fiancé had just told them. Right under their noses – their John Doe had been right under their noses all this time. How could anyone not have known?

But wait, there are about 500 people working in this building, he told himself. He knew a fair few of them, but he couldn't know them all. But to have him here... right here... it defied belief.

Yet, if he was such the computer wizard that Sean said he was, then he could have easily been running the shots all the time by directing them to crime scenes and falsifying his identity to that of a man lying comatose in the hospital. That would have been a piece of cake for him to do.

And no wonder he stole Monica Williams's phone, once he knew she had a picture of him. And wiped her cloud storage at the same time. He couldn't have known about the external hard drive backup though, which was a blessing.

Burton was just grateful that Sean had finished his shift at the same time as his fiancée tonight and he was more than grateful that his eagle eyes had spotted the picture. What were the odds of that happening? Burton couldn't imagine, but he was glad that today, of all days, Sean's and Jane Francis's shifts coincided.

After about twenty minutes, Wayman finally returned to the incident room. 'Got it!' he declared, waving a piece of paper in his hand.

'Right,' Burton said, grabbing it from him. 'Wayman, you're with me, and ring down to the desk to get a couple of uniforms to come with us. I don't think that he'll be wanting to come along willingly.'

* * *

With instructions for the lights and sirens to be extinguished, they made a quiet approach to the address in Withington. The brick-fronted building looked like it had at one time been one two-storey house, but had since been divided into flats. All four men left the car and made their way up the gravel drive where Burton pressed the buzzer for flat four. No reply. He gave it a couple more buzzes before trying another flat. Number two answered almost immediately. A young man's voice said, 'Hello.'

'I'm DI Burton from Manchester City Police and I'm trying to locate Rob Pratchett. I believe he lives at number four?'

'He did,' the man said, 'but he moved out on Saturday morning.

Didn't have much from all accounts as I think he was only working down here for a short while.'

'Do you mind if we come up and have a word, sir,' Burton pushed to get them all in the building.

'Sure, of course.' Burton pushed the door inwards when the buzzer sounded to open the door, closely followed by Wayman and the uniforms.

'Yes, that's Rob,' the young man, who introduced himself as Frank Downs, told them on seeing Rob's photograph. 'He only moved in about six weeks ago, but he said that it was only a temporary contract he was working on and that he'd be leaving to go back home at the end of that time.'

'Where was back home?' Burton asked, notebook at the ready.

'Not sure, really, but somewhere up north. I think I heard a fair bit of Geordie in his accent, though. It is quite distinctive, isn't it?'

'Did anybody come to visit him when he was here?' Burton was hoping that this Pratchett person was not a loner and that he did have memorable visitors.

'Just his girlfriend. I never saw anybody else coming in, but then I'm not usually in until after five during the week.'

'What did the girlfriend look like?'

'I can show you,' Downs said, reaching for his phone out the back pocket of his jeans, then stopped short. 'Now this is not how it looks,' he said almost apologetically.

'What do you mean?'

'I saw them together a few times, thought she was pretty hot like, and one day when she left, I took a photo of her getting into the car.'

'Have you taken many pictures of this person?' Burton asked, knowing that repeatedly taking pictures of someone without their permission could be seen as harassment and could get them into trouble.

'Er... no.' Downs seemed unsure, which made Burton think that it may not have been just the one.

'Okay, let's have a look. Just make sure you don't make a habit of it in future.'

'I won't, detective. There she is,' Downs said, holding up a picture of a woman getting into her car. She must have seen him taking the photograph as she was looking directly up at the lens, and not looking too happy about it either. But it wasn't her expression that interested him, it was her face.

'I think I heard him call her Carol, or something like that,' Downs offered, trying to be helpful, or trying to make amends for his perceived indiscretion.

'No, it wasn't Carol,' Burton told him, 'it was Claire.' He took the phone off the man and showed it to his DC. The woman in the picture was Claire Rawlins.

27

S ally Fielding could hear voices moving around her. She was cold, she was shivering, and she knew that she was no longer in the warmth of the house. The voices sounded as if they were at the bottom of a well or far away at the end of a very long tunnel. A man's voice and a woman's voice, both talking.

Where was she? What was happening? She could feel something rough tied around her eyes, she couldn't tell exactly what it was, but knew it was there to stop her from seeing where she was. It smelled of damp, of earth, and it felt like it was out of doors somewhere. She couldn't feel her arms or her legs no matter how much she tried, only the blindfold around her eyes.

'I think she's coming round,' the man's voice said. 'She's been out a bit longer than I'd expected.'

Then the woman's voice joined his. 'I must have given her a bit too much then.'

'You're supposed to be the one with medical training!' His voice was angry. 'You could have killed her by giving her an overdose.'

'I gave her enough to knock her out.' Her response was equally angry. 'I know what I'm doing. Do you think we've come this far for me to kill her before we're done with her?'

Recognising who the female was, Fielding finally managed to find her voice. 'Claire... what's going on?'

'Finally,' the man said. 'She's back with us.'

She felt hands at the back of her head untying her eye covering. Her sight was at first blurry, but she adjusted fairly quickly to the low light. She wasn't outdoors as she'd at first anticipated. She was inside some kind of wooden structure. A battery light hanging on a hook was the only illumination. It revealed Claire Rawlins and the man from the flat.

'What is this?' Fielding struggled in vain with the cable ties on her hands and feet. She knew they were virtually impossible to get off.

'This,' the man said, 'is your fate, your payback.'

'What do you mean?'

He turned to Claire. 'Would you like to explain, or should I?'

She looked at him. 'I think that the pleasure should be yours, don't you?'

'Very well.' He turned to Fielding and said with a smirk, 'Are you sitting comfortably?'

He pulled up one of the folding chairs and sat down directly in front of her, looking her over. 'You don't recognise me, do you?'

Fielding in turn looked at him, at his features, in his eyes. She had no idea who he was, had never seen him before, but as she looked closer, he did bear a slight resemblance to their sketch of John Doe. But their John Doe had had hair, whereas this man now seated before her only had a slight stubble all over his head, and he didn't have any facial hair.

But what could he possibly want with her, and what was Claire Rawlins doing here with him?

'I think we've been looking for you,' she said. 'You know Alex Carruthers, don't you?'

He laughed. 'Him? He was a means to an end, and this is the end.'

Fielding knew she was centre stage in the whole course of events, the main player. But she couldn't figure out how she had become this. Was it to do with one of her cases? Was it something to do with her life back in the north east? *He's got a bit of a Geordie accent...* she thought. 'I don't understand.'

He sat back and folded his arms. 'Then let me explain.'

Claire pulled up another seat and sat alongside him.

'Do you remember when we were at school...'

'We?' said Fielding. 'I don't know you from school!'

'Oh yes you do,' interrupted Claire. 'Everybody knew him... and his brother... because of you and your two stupid little friends.'

So this was what all of this was about, something to do with her school days? 'My friends? Do you mean Jennifer and Caroline? Did you have something to do with their deaths?'

'For a police officer, you're really not all that bright, are you?' Claire said to Fielding. 'Not very bright at all. Have you not cottoned on to this yet?'

'But I don't know him,' Fielding protested again. 'I neither know him nor his brother.'

'Will you stop saying that!' the man shouted. 'Rob and Jonathan Pratchett... know the names now?'

Fielding was silent. She had to think, but yes, she did remember the names now, and they brought back memories long forgotten. The boys had been sixteen when they arrived in Boldon, just around the same time that Claire had done, and they hadn't just been brothers, they were twins. They had both been plus size, as she recalled, and other children in the school had taunted them about this. She remembered because they'd been referred to as Tweedledee and Tweedledum, two characters from the Lewis Carroll books. At the time, she and her two friends were into anything to do with Alice and her adventures and had their own little 'Wonderland' gang. Naturally, she was 'Alice', Caroline had been the 'Queenie' and Jennifer 'Hattie'. It was a possibility that the name-callers had picked up on this for obvious reasons, but in reality, it had nothing to do with them. Surely they weren't being held responsible for that, were they?

'I still don't understand,' she said. 'What does this have to do with me or my friends, we didn't call either you or your brother names?'

Pratchett looked over towards Rawlins and back to Fielding again. 'You're kidding, right?'

Fielding shook her head. She really had no idea, despite what he thought. 'Did you kill all those people?' she asked.

Claire exchanged glances with Rob Pratchett and smiled, saying, 'That was a joint effort.'

'But why?' Fielding tried to discreetly work at her ties as she kept them talking. But she was not as discreet as she'd thought and Pratchett had seen what she was doing. He brought two more cable ties out of his jacket, slipped them on and pulled them tighter than before. They dug into her and she flinched with the pain.

Claire continued as if nothing had happened. 'Your profiler was correct in that all the victims were not the intended ones. The only ones we wanted to die were you and your friends.'

'But what about Alex Carruthers?'

'Just a pawn in our game,' Pratchett laughed, 'and he fulfilled his purpose. Then we made him the prime suspect, didn't we?'

'But the other three people... they were innocent. Why did they have to die?' Fielding couldn't budge the new ties no matter how hard she tried while keeping them talking.

'They weren't so innocent,' said Pratchett. 'We found out things about them that made them guilty. Guilty of not speaking up when they saw abuse in the schools they worked in. Turning a blind eye to children being taunted, just like you and your friends taunted me and Jonathan. So not so innocent.'

'Why the sudden urgency to get "payback" as you call it?'

Pratchett stood up and put both hands on the back of the chair and stared at her with an intensity she found disconcerting – even more so than the position she had found herself in now. 'Because,' he said, eyes not blinking or leaving hers, 'Jonathan killed himself last year. And you and your friends are to blame.'

'How can we be to blame for something your brother did last year? I haven't seen either of you in over thirteen years and neither my friends nor I taunted either you or your brother. We would never have done that. Surely you haven't been carrying a grudge for all that time for something none of us did? That's just insane.'

'I'm not insane!' Pratchett barked at her, his face so close to hers that she could feel the heat of his breath on her.

'Rob...' Claire put a hand on his shoulder. 'Keep it together.'

He turned around and slapped her hard on the face, causing her to fall to the ground.

'What are you doing?' she cried out, holding her cheek where he'd hit her with his hand. But he ignored her and turned his attention back to Fielding again.

'You three bitches drove my brother insane. He was never the same after the name-calling he got from all of you. Spent most of his time in and out of institutions after that. You had no idea what you did to him... and me, but I had the strength to fight it and I swore that one day I would get my own back on all of you – for Jonathan. Claire here... my lovely Claire... she helped me, she was here for me, and she said that she would help me. It was despicable what you did.'

'But it wasn't even us,' Fielding tried to argue with him. But she realised that this hatred he had for her and her friends had been thirteen years in the making and wasn't simply going to go away with her saying a few words of kindness to him.

'Give her another shot, double it this time,' he shouted to Claire. 'I want this over with now.'

'Are you sure?' she questioned him.

Is she having doubts perhaps now that she is facing the reality of the situation? wondered Fielding. Was the reality of killing someone that she had briefly gelled with again on their trip back up north too much for Claire Rawlins?

Pratchett grabbed her by both shoulders. 'This is what we have been planning for over a year now. If you can't do it, then I will.' He let go of her and strode over towards her bag to get the syringe.

'No... no,' she stopped him. 'I'll do it.'

Fielding saw the syringe getting closer and closer to her skin, then felt it sink deep into the muscle of her upper arm. It stung for a few seconds, then she felt her head begin to spin and her head dropped heavily down onto her chest.

28

Burton dialled Fielding's phone for the fifth time – still going to voicemail.

'Do we know where Claire Rawlins is staying?' he shouted frantically to anyone who would listen, but nobody had an answer for him. 'Have a look on Fielding's desk,' he shouted over to Summers, 'see if you can find the card that she gave her.'

Dammit, she contacted us, Burton thought, *not the other way around*, realising that this had been planned for a very long time, her and this Rob Pratchett. But why? As far as he knew, neither his name nor Claire Rawlins's name had popped up in relation to any of Fielding's past cases. This had to be something personal between them.

Then he remembered Dr Barnes at the coroner's office. Surely he would have contact details for Rawlins as she had been working there. He found the number for the coroner's office in his contact list and dialled. When the girl on the switchboard told him that Dr Barnes had left for the evening, Burton insisted that she give him either his home or mobile number. She refused him on the basis of confidentiality. It was then that he lost his patience with her and threatened legal action if she did not comply.

There was a pause. 'I'm going to pass you to my line manager.'

And after a brief but fired discussion – with another threat of court action and anything else he could throw at her – Burton was finally given Dr Barnes's mobile number.

'She said that she had been called back to her office in the north east,' Dr Barnes told him, 'and cleared out her locker at lunchtime. What's happening?'

Not wanting to go into the full details, Burton simply explained that they urgently needed information from her on the case they were working on. 'And do you have an address for her?'

'Well I don't, I'm afraid.' It wasn't the answer Burton had hoped for. 'But HR will have it... I'll give you their extension number.' Burton could hear the sound of him turning pages. 'Here we are,' he said at last. 'HR are the same number as you dialled to get me, but then it's extension 4421. There should be somebody still there as I believe that they work up to 7pm.'

Burton steeled himself to go through the whole process once again. But he got the same girl on the switchboard as before. She didn't waste any time in putting him through to HR. The man he spoke to was very helpful, going out of his way to be of assistance. But he came back with the information Burton neither expected nor wanted.

The address he provided for Claire Rawlins was that of Rob Pratchett's temporary apartment in Withington.

This wasn't the way Sally Fielding had envisaged herself going out. Lying in a bed somewhere, surrounded by children and grandchildren, having lived a long and happy life – that was how she'd thought that her story would have ended.

But no, here she was tied up and sitting on the cold, damp floor of what seemed to be a shed in somebody's back garden. Or an allotment maybe? Was that where she was, in Jacob Stephenson's shed in his allotment? She could see the irony in that.

Claire Rawlins and her boyfriend, Rob Pratchett, would have been highly amused by that final kick in the teeth – depositing their final victim at the crime scene for one of their other victims. Who would have ever thought to look for her there? Her phone wasn't even turned on. They'd both made sure that it was turned off when they left her to her fate. And there it was, lying on the ground some distance away from her, too far for her to reach and turn on again. Taunting her, like some in her school had taunted Rob Pratchett and his twin brother, Jonathan. They would have thought that to be fitting and apt.

And she was cold, freezing in fact. They hadn't even given her the courtesy of putting her coat back on her, and all she had on was a tunic top, a fairly thin one at that, and a pair of leggings and ankle boots. They wouldn't be enough to protect her when the temperature dropped even further during the night. She closed her eyes and thought about all the things that she would miss – her cats, her work, Joe Burton.

She also regretted not making things up with her mother and sister. It seemed to her that she would not have the chance to now. Then there was the card she was looking at right beside her mobile phone – the queen of hearts, exactly the same as the ones found by the dead bodies of her old school friends.

* * *

Joe Burton was frantic, and that sense of desperation was spilling over to his team. He had called DCI Ambleton to tell her the news and she had dropped everything and set off for the station immediately after his call to her had ended.

'What can we do?' Burton paced the floor in his own office while the DCI was sitting on the sofa in the corner. 'Her phone is turned off so we can't track it, I don't know what else we can do to find her.'

Ambleton could see the look of frustration and despondency on his face for his second-in-command, who was not merely another police officer to him. Sally Fielding had had his back on so many occasions, and likewise he'd had hers. They were the best team pairing she had known since she herself had partnered with Burton back in the day. But it wasn't just professional courtesy that was driving him on, for she knew that he held quite strong feelings for his colleague, even though he would never let on the fact that he did. He felt that a workplace just wasn't the place for any romantic entanglement, despite what he might feel beneath the detached exterior he constantly maintained. The truth was, he was more than fond of her, and in any other circumstances, would have made a move on her long before now. But in a job like theirs, there was no place for distractions... of any kind.

'There's absolutely no way of tracking a phone that's off, is there?' DCI Ambleton came up with the suggestion, but knew in her heart that she was clutching at straws. She knew for a fact that a phone had to be turned on in order to track it, but with today's technology, surely there must be a way to find her? 'There must be something on her that we can track. Can we not get our tech guys on this, Burton?'

Burton had sat down at his desk and had his head in his hands. 'No, there's nothing, absolutely nothing. The only tech thing I know that she has, apart from her phone, is her activity watch. But we don't even know if she would be wearing that tonight.'

DCI Ambleton had a thought. 'Has she been wearing it regularly recently?'

Burton had to think about it, and remembered what she'd said about going out for a jog on the Sunday morning, how she'd decided to wear it every day now. 'I think she had started to,' he told her.

'Do you know if those watches have GPS on them?'

Burton gave that a thought, then something occurred to him. 'Oh, boss, you're brilliant,' he said, jumping to his feet. 'I'm not enough of a computer tech expert to know that, but I know somebody downstairs in the cells who is.'

* * *

'Yes, it's possible,' Alex Carruthers said when he was sitting in an interview room with both Burton and Ambleton. 'As long as it's being worn, that is, and the battery is still viable.'

Burton looked at his boss. 'So we've only really got until the battery runs out, and we don't know how long's left on it.' That was something that they hadn't considered, the length of time left before Fielding's watch would run out of charge and turn itself off for good. And if they hadn't found her by then, well that would be it. They'd never be able to find her and they'd be too late. She'd be gone.

'We don't even know if she's wearing it, Joe.' Ambleton hated to say it but felt that she had to.

'We must assume that she is.'

'But what if she's not,' she had started to say to him.

Burton felt his heart pounding against his ribs. He felt as if he was going to have a coronary; he was getting that worked up. 'We have to, because that's all the hope that we have.' He was practically shouting at her. His face felt hot and he could sense beads of sweat on his forehead.

Ambleton, concerned for his welfare, looked at Carruthers and said, 'Just how do we do this then?'

'I'll need access to a computer,' he said, 'and the information about her watch. Does this now mean that I am off the hook?' Carruthers added after a slight pause.

Burton had already sprinted out of the door, leaving his boss to answer the question for him.

'Yes, it does,' she told him.

29

Burton and Fielding had agreed a very long time ago that each should have a key to the other's homes in case of a situation like this.

The cats made a beeline for him when he came in. He didn't feel he had the time to stop and pet them, but he knew what they meant to her, so he quickly bent down to stroke them before starting his search for the activity watch box. Carruthers had told them that in order to do a sweep to find her, he would need to have the serial number of the device and the exact make and model.

Burton was now getting heart palpitations. He knew that he should try to slow down a little bit, but time was running out and he needed to find this as soon as he possibly could. Where would she put it, where? He looked everywhere: in the sideboard drawers in the living room, in the chest of drawers in the bedroom, he even looked in the vanity unit under the sink in the bathroom, but nothing.

Not one to ever get emotional to the point where he would find himself welling up with tears, he was now on the brink of breaking down and sobbing his heart out. It was then that he found it, hiding in plain sight – well almost – on the floor beneath the dining table right next to the cats' beds. They must have been playing with it in her absence. Quickly checking that the box had all the information that he needed, he took his phone out of his pocket, took a photo of it then messaged it on to Ambleton, hands trembling as he did so.

* * *

Back at the station, Ambleton was still sitting in his office with Carruthers seated at his desk in front of his computer. This was not the picture he could have imagined a few hours ago when the man was down in the cells and about to be charged for the murder of at least three, and probably five, people.

Instead, here he was now, about to find Sally.

While Carruthers got to work, Burton felt like the whole world was collapsing around him. He could hardly get his breath he was that worked up. Carruthers had been working for less than fifteen minutes and it was already fifteen minutes too long for him. Burton needed to find her now... right now.

'Burton, why don't you go grab yourself a coffee,' DCI Ambleton suggested, seeing the state he was getting himself into. 'I'm sure Mr Carruthers here is going as quickly as he can.'

Even though the idea of drinking greyish-beige station coffee was the last thing on his mind, he decided to grab a small one and get some fresh air as well at the same time. The canteen had a small balcony where people went out to grab a quick smoke or vape, and although he was the only one out there at this time of night, he could still smell the cigarette butts reeking in the waste bins. Burton was glad that he'd never succumbed to the habit, although there had been many occasions when he could have willingly lit up to take the edge off things. This was one of them.

He took a sip of the coffee. It was as disgusting as he'd expected, but he still drank it anyway, swallowing it down with the reluctance of a child being force-fed a meal. He completely lost track of the time as he watched the evening traffic flow by in the streets below him. The city was starting to get busy again. Gone was the five o'clock rush hour, to be replaced by the evening one, where people were going out for the evening to clubs, cinemas, theatres or restaurants. Going out to meet their friends and loved ones, to enjoy themselves and be happy – all except him. He was just standing there watching them, observing the scene play out around him, and feeling completely lost and unable to do anything about it. Then his phone rang in his pocket. He looked at the screen: Ambleton.

'You'd better get back here quickly.' Her voice was hurried and hoarse, as if she'd already been screaming orders around the incident room. He didn't hesitate.

Alex Carruthers had to confess that tracking a person's location by the GPS on their activity watch was in its infancy stage. However, he had managed to do it. He had traced the watch to Foxfield Road Allotments.

'Isn't that where the body of Jacob Stephenson was found?' Wayman said.

'Get a car out front... now,' Burton screamed to nobody in particular, and Summers flew out of the room as quickly as he could.

DCI Ambleton took Burton's arm. 'You know, Joe,' she said in almost a whisper, 'I hate to say this, but it might just be the watch there, and not Fielding. This could just be a red herring and she might not even be there.'

'I know that,' he said, almost hysterical now, and Ambleton could see a tear running down his cheek, 'but we've got to try, haven't we? It's all we have to go on.'

'I know,' she said, letting go of him. 'You'd better hurry then. I'll stay with here with Carruthers while you're gone.' And with that he was out of the door, hot on Summers's tail and grabbing Wayman by the arm as he passed him.

'Let's hope she's there,' Carruthers said to her, looking at the location still flashing on the computer screen in front of him.

'Yes, let's,' was all she could manage to say.

* * *

Burton was counting the seconds, never mind the minutes, as the car weaved in and out of the traffic, lights flashing and sirens going, and it wasn't going fast enough for him.

'Put your foot down, man,' he shouted at the driver, a uniformed police officer who looked nervously at his superior and squirmed uncomfortably in his seat, not knowing quite how to answer his request when he knew it wasn't safe to do what he was being asked.

'I'm going as fast as I safely can, sir,' he apologised, fearful that he was heading for some official reprimand if he didn't put his foot down and speed up like his superior officer had demanded.

'Boss,' Summers jumped in to try and defuse the situation, which showed all the signs of escalating. He put a hand on Burton's arm. 'He's doing his best, and we're almost there.'

The car made a quick swerve right then left and Burton recognised the road that led to the lane alongside the allotments. The car had barely stopped when he flung the door open and began to run along to where he knew Jacob Stephenson's plot was. Wayman and Summers started off behind him, but Burton's adrenalin was already geared up to an all-time high and he was already some distance ahead of them on the lane.

The shed was in darkness when Burton reached it and no light or sounds were coming from it or from anywhere nearby. There was a heavy-duty padlock on the door and he desperately looked around for something to prise it open with.

'Help me find something,' he shouted to the other two detectives, who produced their torches and scanned the beam around the surroundings. There was nothing to be found anywhere.

'Run back to the car, one of you, and see what's in the boot that can get this thing off.' Summers started off back down the lane, returning a few minutes later with a tyre wrench and a set of screwdrivers. 'That's all there is,' he began, but Burton grabbed the wrench away from him and began to whack the padlock with it. As it was having no effect, Wayman stepped in and started to undo the screws on the hasp with an unsteady hand. He was shaking like a leaf, fully aware of the urgency of the situation. It eventually fell off and landed on the ground and Burton threw his entire body weight against the door and fell into the shed, landing beside Fielding's motionless body.

30
_____

I t was all over the newspapers the next day: Body found in allotment shed in Manchester named as Detective Sergeant Alice S. Fielding.

Claire Rawlins was sitting having breakfast in her kitchen diner back up in Whitley Bay when she heard her boyfriend put his key in the front door.

'Where are you?' he shouted as he came in waving a newspaper. He slapped it down on the table in front of her. 'Look at this!' he said proudly, pointing to the headline and accompanying photograph of the woman he had hated for over thirteen years.

'You've done it,' she told him, looking at the picture of her one-time friend. The photograph the police force had provided the press with was one of her in full uniform. It looked like it had been taken at an award ceremony of some kind.

'No. We've done it,' he corrected her, bending over and kissing the top of her head. 'And it feels good, doesn't it?'

She really didn't know what to say to him. After all this time, after all the planning and scheming they'd done, it suddenly felt flat somehow, as if there should have been fireworks and champagne and celebrations. But in truth, there was nothing. Claire felt unrewarded somehow.

'Hey, honey, what's wrong?' Pratchett asked, sensing that she was nowhere near as happy as he was at that moment. 'We knew that it wasn't going to be easy, didn't we? But the crimes we've committed to get here have been far more gruesome than giving somebody a fatal overdose.'

She smiled at him. 'It's just...' but she was interrupted by the sound of the doorbell.

'Are you expecting somebody?' he asked her.

'No,' she said, getting up from her chair. 'I didn't tell anybody that I was coming back yet.'

As she went to find out who it was, Pratchett poured himself a cup of coffee from the machine on the kitchen worktop. Despite his girlfriend's reaction to the news, he was feeling on top of the world, never better. His twin brother would be so proud of him right now. Yes, he'd done him proud; done both of them proud. He sat down at the table and looked at the newspaper headlines again, taking the reality of it all in. He had just downed his second mouthful of coffee when he thought he saw movement in the hedge at the bottom of the garden. He got up and walked over to the patio doors and looked out, but whatever it was had long gone by the time he got there. *Probably just a cat walking on the fence,* he thought to himself, but as he kept looking, he saw in the window the reflection of the door from the living room opening. Thinking it was Claire coming back from seeing who was at the front door, he turned around, and at that moment the door burst open and Detective Inspector Burton and a team of armed police officers came tearing in.

'Police! Down on the floor! Hands behind your head!' several voices all shouted out to him at once, and without hesitation, Rob Pratchett threw himself on the floor and did as he was told, clasping both of his hands behind him at the back of his neck.

'Robert Pratchett,' Burton began while the other officers were putting handcuffs on him, 'I'm arresting you for the murders of Jennifer Grayson, Caroline Porter, Nathaniel Jackson, Jacob Stephenson and Dorothy Johnson. You do not have to say anything, but it may harm your defence if you do not mention when questioned something which you later rely on in court. Anything you do say may be given in evidence.'

Pratchett was then hauled up onto his feet and taken into the living room where Claire Rawlins was already seated on the sofa with an officer on either side of her. She was red-eyed and had already been handcuffed. She looked up at him as he entered with an expression of sheer desperation. But Burton had one last thing to say to both of them before they were taken off to the nearest police station. 'And,' he said, staring at Pratchett and then Rawlins with firm, unyielding eyes, 'for the attempted murder of Detective Sergeant Sally Fielding.'

Pratchett's face went the colour of washed-out clay.

Detective Sergeant Sally Fielding finally gained consciousness and began to stir. As she opened her eyes, they took the full blast of the sun which was pouring in through the gap in the blinds on the huge picture window directly across from her. She squinted and shielded her face against the brightness, and as her hand went up to her eyes, she also took a collection of wires and electrodes attached to her finger with it. The machine behind her started to beep urgently. She could see that she was in a hospital; not in a ward but in a room on her own. Her head felt fuzzy and heavy, and she had a crashing headache. She tried hard to remember what had happened that had brought her to this place but her mind and thoughts were all jumbled up and she couldn't think clearly.

'Ah, you're awake,' a nurse appeared by her side as if from nowhere and smiled at her, reattaching her electrodes and silencing the machine's beeping. 'There are a lot of people who will be thrilled that you're finally back with us. Now, just take it easy and I'll get you something to drink. Do you feel up to trying a little bit of food as well?'

Fielding felt pains in her stomach at the mention of food. She had no idea how long it had been since she had last eaten, so she said that she would try.

With an, 'Okay, I'll see what I can do,' the nurse breezed out of the room as quickly as she had appeared. Fielding could hear her stop and talk to somebody directly outside of her room, then the sound of her feet moving further away along the corridor. It was some time later, when she was sitting with a sandwich and a glass of water on the tray table, that the door reopened and in came Burton with a huge smile across his face.

'You look a bit better than when I saw you last,' he laughed, bending forward to give her a kiss on the forehead.

'I just can't quite remember what happened,' she confessed. She'd been trying to get her head around the order of events all morning, but couldn't seem to get past sitting with Claire Rawlins in her living room and drinking the wine she'd brought for them. She thought that a man might have come in, but other than that her memory was a blank.

'Do you want me to tell you,' Burton asked. 'Or have the doctors said that it's better for you to remember things on your own?'

Fielding sat up a bit further against the pillow. 'Nobody has spoken to me about it yet, but yes, I'd like you to tell me.'

As Burton related the events of what had happened two days prior to today, Fielding just couldn't believe what she was hearing. All these murders had been about what had been said to a couple of overweight boys back in high school? It hadn't even been her and her friends who had said it.

'I suppose I can see in their twisted minds why they killed the women up in Boldon, but why kill these three people in Manchester as well?'

Burton wasn't sure if she was asking herself this out loud or if she was asking him for an answer, but he replied anyway.

'Well, they were trying to frame Alex Carruthers for his great-uncle's death, and the other two killings were red herrings to throw us off – although, Pratchett did admit that they'd been chosen because of their link to education. Likewise with your two old friends. He had hoped that Carruthers's job taking him up there during the week would make him the obvious person of interest. And it would have worked as well if we didn't have the final break-through with our own DC Francis's fiancé recognising him. Can you believe that he was working upstairs in our building all this time?'

'So, in effect, he was keeping tabs on us all the time?' she said.

'Yes, him and Rawlins.'

Fielding thought about that for a moment. 'So did she kill the two girls?' Burton nodded. After the arrest at Claire Rawlins's home in Whitley Bay the previous morning they had both confessed everything. Rawlins had committed the two murders on Tyneside and Pratchett the ones in Manchester.

They had tried to get Fielding to realise her connection to the crimes by leaving the playing cards beside the bodies, but what they had failed to realise – or had chosen not to – was that her link had only been a very tenuous one. Yes, she did remember the twins and the fact that one of them had been hospitalised during the summer holidays after leaving school, but she had no idea why that was. She was far too busy preparing to move away to college and away from her family to wonder what had become of all those in her peer group. Although she'd chosen to use her middle name of Sally when leaving school instead of her given first name of Alice, this was nothing to do with school, it was simply her way of breaking away and making a fresh start for herself in Manchester, away from her disapproving family. In any case, she would never have recognised either of them after all that time; she'd barely recognised Claire when she saw her again.

'By the way,' Burton changed the subject, 'Simon Banks is coming out today. Taking a few weeks' sick leave to get himself back on his feet again. He's in this hospital a couple of floors up.'

Fielding smiled. 'I'm pleased to hear that. So was that Pratchett who attacked him as well?'

'Yes,' Burton told her. 'The photograph taken was one of Carruthers with a group of his computer course graduates, and he was on it. Carruthers apparently gave it to him some time ago. There's something else I think I should mention too. The syringe we found behind you had quite of bit of the drug that they were going to finish you off with left in it. When I questioned Rawlins about it, she said that she just couldn't put all of it in you. She just gave you enough to make you unconscious. No offence, but that's an odd thing to do: suddenly get a conscience after already bumping a couple of people off. Beheading one of them as well.'

Fielding agreed that it was odd considering the circumstances. 'So why were the victims killed in the manner that they were, did they say?'

'Yes they did,' Burton told her. 'And it's all quite bizarre, but makes perfect sense when you know the reasoning behind it.' He then went on to tell her each in turn. 'They were all linked to your favourite Lewis Carroll books, and it was Pratchett's way of trying to get you to realise who was committing the murders.'

Fielding interrupted. 'But did he not realise that neither I nor my friends called them names, it was some of the other pupils?'

'Apparently not it seems, but it was all to punish you and your friends as he saw you three as ringleaders. Being called those names, and knowing what your group was based on, he blamed it all on you all for instigating it.'

'But all those innocent people...'

'I know,' he said. 'But that's what murderers do, isn't it? They kill innocent people all the time and don't think twice about it.'

He gave her a moment before continuing with the reasons. 'Jennifer Grayson, beheaded, and a queen of hearts card beside her.'

'Off with their head,' Fielding murmured to herself.

'Caroline Porter was found head down in a planter with the same card, but what the photographs didn't show us was that the planter she was found in was a large tea cup and saucer.'

'Oh no,' Fielding said, realising the significance of that. 'The tea party.'

'And then Mr Jackson dressed in what we initially thought was a clown outfit, but Pratchett said he was supposed to look like the Mad Hatter. He thought that we'd get that instantly, especially with the link to the tannin poisoning which is something that is found in tea. He was quite disappointed that we didn't get that one. The joker card seemed appropriate, he said. Then Mr Stephenson died with a mouthful of sweets which, if you look at them very carefully – and I've since looked at the ME photos – are tiny caterpillars. The king of spades had a gardening connotation. And finally, Dorothy Johnson, beaten to death with a mallet. Pratchett said he couldn't get his hands on a croquet mallet, but found a very good wooden one that did the trick. Charming man.'

'That's just so sick.' Fielding had trouble digesting all of this. This had all happened because some people had inappropriately named the twin brothers at school after characters in a book? Unfortunately, the same series of books that she and her friends had named their little group after. What sort of warped mind devised a plan like that? It was a lot to take in, and she sat staring into the distance, stunned by what she'd just been told.

Burton gave her some time before continuing, 'When you're better, I'll show you your obituary in the papers.'

'My what!' she exclaimed. That brought her back to earth with a bang.

'We had to make Pratchett and Rawlins think that they'd killed you as well in Jacob Stephenson's shed. We knew that they would think that they'd gotten away scot-free, and we suspected that both of them would be heading off up north to Claire's place in Whitley Bay. I'm so glad that you told me about that place, otherwise it might have taken us quite some time to find her. So we arranged with the local press to run the story of your death. It was quite a gamble as we didn't really know if either of them would buy a newspaper, but we figured that they might want to see the results of all their work, so it paid off.'

'My death was in the local press up there?' Fielding was shocked. Although she no longer had any connection to the place, her immediate thoughts went to her mother and her sister and how they would react to seeing something like that.

'It's okay, it's okay, don't worry.' Burton got up from his seat and reassured her, sensing that she was becoming agitated as the beeping on her monitor had begun to increase quite rapidly. 'In fact, I'm going to just step out for a moment as I know that there's somebody here who wants to see you.'

'No, I'm okay,' she said, reaching out to try to stop him from leaving, thinking that he was going in search of a doctor, but he just smiled and opened the door then walked through it. She heard a murmur of voices outside in the corridor before the door opened again. When it did, Fielding saw two people walk through it who she had never expected to ever see again. Two people who she had turned her back on when they had all fallen out with one another. Two people who Burton had forewarned about the newspaper report and had brought back down to Manchester with him the previous day – her mother and her sister.

ACKNOWLEDGMENTS

After not writing anything for four years, when fellow North East writer and Bloodhound Books author, AM Peacock, drew my attention to a local short story competition, I thought that I would try to get into storytelling again. So my grateful thanks go to Adam for mentioning this and for inspiring me to try my hand at crime writing, something which I had never attempted before.

I will be eternally grateful to Bloodhound Books and to Betsy for giving me this opportunity, and for having faith in me and my writing. I would also like to thank my editor, Clare Law, as well as Heather Fitt, Sumaira Wilson and Tara Lyons for their continued support and guidance.

Also, Christine Naylor, thank you for your continued support and encouragement. Who would have thought when we were working together in South Shields library in the dim distant past that I'd end up writing a book myself?

A special mention must go to Heather Rutherford who, all those years ago when we were in our teens, was my writing buddy. She is, and always will be, my oldest friend.

Last, but by no means least, in memory of those no longer here: Gladys Maddison, Colin Murray, Jack Murray and Kath Murray. Gone but not forgotten. I would have loved you all to have read it.

Printed in Great
Britain
by Amazon